# DEADLOCK

*To my wife Anna, with love and thanks*

# DEADLOCK

*by*

## Jack Holt

**Dales Large Print Books**
Long Preston, North Yorkshire,
BD23 4ND, England.

**British Library Cataloguing in Publication Data.**

Holt, Jack
    Deadlock.

    A catalogue record of this book is
    available from the British Library

    ISBN   1–84262–302–8 pbk

First published in Great Britain in 2003 by Robert Hale Ltd.

Published in Large Print 2004 by arrangement with
Robert Hale Ltd.

Dales Large Print is an imprint of Library Magna Books Ltd.

Printed and bound in Great Britain by
T.J. (International) Ltd., Cornwall, PL28 8RW

# CHAPTER ONE

They came out of the desert, five riders, collectively known as the Brodie gang. Their objective was the bank at Gila Junction. The fly trap town had previously not attracted bank robbers, because the take would normally be meagre. The reason for the Brodie gang's interest now, arose from a conversation which Gabby Scanell, the gang's cook and general dogsbody, had lip read between two men in a saloon in Hadley Wells, a much more prosperous town ten miles north of Gila junction. Their talk was about a cash shipment that would be lodged in the Gila junction bank for some days, awaiting transit to a mining company close to the Mexican border.

Gabby Scanell's talent for lip reading had been perfected as a young man when he had courted a deaf girl for a spell before hitting the owlhoot trail. His ability had, over the years, served the gang well, giving them information which no one suspected they had. It was a skill which had saved Cy

7

Brodie's life when his luck at cards was misinterpreted, and a sore loser sought to retrieve his losses by slitting Cy's throat.

Cy Brodie owed Gabby Scanell for that.

At first, Gila Junction seemed an unlikely stopover for the shipment of cash. Logic would have suggested that either Hadley Wells or a town called Bowen Crossing, (a town Cy Brodie knew very well, and its no-nonsense lawman Bob Latchford better still) should have been the choice. But when thought through, the sense of using the Gila junction bank became clear. While there was a risk that some outfit might raid the bank at Hadley Wells or Bowen Crossing, who would suspect such riches would be found in the Gila Junction bank?

The plan was to ship the money in crates mixed in with goods destined for the general store in Gila Junction, transported as common freight. There was a chance, of course, that freight might be stolen too, but the risk was minimal. Whereas a high-profile, guarded shipment would attract lots of attention – all bad.

It was a clever plan.

Through some shrewd detective work, Cy Brodie had discovered that the two men talking in the Hadley Wells saloon were

8

Benjamin Bowles the mining company president, and Ethan Briscoe the president of the Gila Junction bank.

Briscoe had said, 'The less ballyhoo the better. I'll just lock up as normal and go on home.'

Even the Gila Junction sheriff was to be kept in the dark.

When Bowles had expressed his reservations about keeping the law in the dark, Briscoe's reasoning was: 'The less who know the better.'

Of course, there were some who would have to be in the know, Ethan Briscoe had explained. Like the owner of the general store and a few more of the bank president's friends.

'All men who are utterly trustworthy,' Briscoe had reassured the worried mining company president.

During the long and often sleepless nights on the trail, Cy Brodie had dreamed the outlaws' dream of striking it rich and quitting. Bull Rankin, a natural insomniac, would sometimes dream along with him, but their plans were radically different.

'I'd head east,' Rankin would dream. 'Where a man can make his fortune fast.'

Cy Brodie's dream was to ranch in the

9

sweet grass country of Montana, where seasons changed and where leaves turned to gold in the fall, and the smell of woodsmoke would fill the air. Where the earth under a man's feet would be soft and yielding, unlike the rocky, parched land he now walked on.

Their dreaming would always end the same way with Rankin saying, 'There's no way out of this kind of life, Cy. We're deadlocked.'

Cy Brodie's gaze went Gabby Scanell's way. His jaded look worried the gang leader. Scanell, in his late fifties, was too old to be part of any outfit. Living rough and always sleeping with one eye open took its toll on a man, particularly an oldster like Gabby Scanell. But Gabby had nowhere else to go, and would ride with the gang until he fell out of his saddle, or caught lead. If the pickings were as rich as forecast in the Gila Junction raid, maybe he could quit. Maybe, Cy Brodie thought, that he could quit too.

Some men were born outlaws, and some, like Brodie, had become outlaws by ill-fortune.

Arriving at sunset, the gang held back until the Gila Junction lights went out, and the only one remaining was the storm lantern over the livery gate. It was thirty after midnight when they rode in. Their horses, trained not to make a sound, passed soundlessly along Main. The night was still, except for a whispering breeze that rocked the livery storm lantern, creating dancing shadows.

Cy Brodie directed his horse along an alley that led to the rear of the bank.

'Wait,' he instructed the others.

He prised open a window and entered the bank. He waited in the darkness. Listened. Brodie still found it hard to believe that the kind of cash they were expecting to find in the bank vault would be left unguarded as part of the plan to prevent attention being drawn to the bank.

He headed for a door marked:

## ETHAN BRISCOE
## PRESIDENT

This would be where the safe was. Palms sweating, Cy Brodie eased open the door, inch by careful inch. Could it be, that after all the lousy hands life had dealt him, he was at last closing in on the pot of all pots?

The room was revealed to him slowly. It held no surprises. There was another door off the office. Maybe that's where the surprise was? The room was poky. A printing press

11

and stacks of paper took up most of it. Cy was curious, but turned his attention to the safe. It was old, and would present no problems for Whistler Long, the gang's safe cracker. Five minutes later they were all crouched behind what cover they could find, waiting for the blast that would unhinge the safe door.

As usual, Gabby Scanell took care of the horses and acted as lookout.

'Might as well be in a darn cemetery,' was one of the gang member's view on Gila Junction.

Whistler Long joked, 'This darn town is so sleepy, Cy, I reckon we could leave some until the morrow for collection.'

But Cy Brodie was acutely conscious of the fact that sometimes it was the quiet towns that raised hell.

There was a bright flash and, despite the sacking which Long had stuffed his charge in, an earth-shattering blast. The bank windows vanished along with a sizeable portion of its side wall. The safe door tilted on twisted hinges. The shock waves were still shaking the bank when the gang looked into the safe at the neat stacks of dollar bills, bound with bands that announced:

## PROPERTY OF THE LONGSHOT
## MINING COMPANY
## NEW MEXICO TERRITORY

'Holy shit!' Whistler Long swore. 'We're rich!'

A gun blasted outside the bank. Gabby Scanell cried out.

'Ride!' Brodie ordered.

The men were caught between saving their hides and grabbing the kind of pot which for years had filled their dreams. Two more shots rang out.

'Now!' Cy added, and dashed to help Gabby Scanell without getting his hands on a single dollar.

Cursing, the others hared after Brodie with only a handful of bills.

Outside, Gabby was on the ground holding his side. Blood seeped through his clutching fingers. A lone shooter was hugging the corner of the bank, six-gun spitting. A trio of shots buzzed around Brodie, biting at the wall of the bank.

Cy's hand dived for his .45, but on the sound of an empty chamber, the man was high-tailing it. Cy held his fire, seeing no point in downing the man now that he had abandoned his attack. He knelt alongside Gabby.

'Can you ride, Gabby?' he asked.

'Get me standin', Cy.'

Brodie helped the oldster up and on to his horse. By now the rest of the gang had already thundered out of town. Windows were lighting up and doors opening.

'The bank's being robbed!' the fleeing shooter was hollering.

'Git, Cy,' Gabby Scanell pleaded. 'Any minute now there'll be guns blasting all over the place.'

Cy said grimly, 'We leave together or not at all, Gabby.'

'Then it will darn well be not at all, I reckon!'

'Grab the saddle horn,' Brodie ordered.

He grabbed the reins of Gabby Scanell's horse. Chased by hot lead, they galloped out of town, risking passage along Main rather than the obstacle-strewn town backlots. The misfortune of a stumbling horse would finish them both.

# CHAPTER TWO

Cy Brodie led the gang into the high country between Gila Junction and Bowen Crossing; country he knew well since his cow-punching days for the Crichton ranch, whose vast range took up a great deal of country between the two towns, and whose expansion was relentless. The ranch was now bossed by Jody Crichton, the late Ned Crichton's son. But Ned Crichton might as well still be around, because Jody was a chip off the old block, every smidgen as mean and conniving as his old man.

It was Ned Crichton's underhandedness that had set Cy Brodie on the owlhoot trail.

Brodie led the way into a canyon Bob Latchford and he had happened upon by chance, and luckily so, when marauding Apaches had given chase. Latchford, now the marshal of Bowen Crossing, had been his range partner in those days. Funny, Cy thought, how life repeats itself. He was again hiding out in the canyon, during the throes of another Apache uprising. Only the

15

last time he did not have a posse on his tail, and a wounded man whose age was working against him.

Gabby Scanell had lost blood, and the hard ride through scorching and torturous terrain had taken its toll. Getting the oldster to the Mexican roost the gang was headed for would present all sorts of risks and danger. His partners, already soured by having to leave behind wealth they would never again set eyes on, were not in an accommodating mood.

'That posse is proving more dogged than we figured on, Cy,' Bull Rankin observed, so called because of his beefy frame and thick short neck. 'Can't figure why they'd punish themselves so, and risk losing their hair for the handful of dollars we heisted?'

Rankin, sometimes a surly and short-tempered man, was the least critical of Cy's diversion to the canyon to allow Gabby Scanell to rest up. The others were for ditching the old man and riding hell for leather for the border.

Brodie agreed with Rankin's assessment of the Gila Junction posse's determination. 'Doesn't make sense, Bull.'

In fact, it bewildered him.

Jack Benteen, a mean-spirited bastard

16

whose only concern, as always, was saving his own hide grumbled, 'I say you've got us in a right bind, Brodie.'

Gabby Scanell defended the gang leader. 'It ain't Cy's fault that I got in the way of a bullet, Benteen.'

Benteen continued with his griping. 'Don't know what an old bastard like you is doin' ridin' with this outfit in the first place, Scanell.'

'Pay no heed, Gabby,' Brodie advised the angry old-timer, as he tried to challenge Benteen. He turned to face Scanell's tormentor, his temper straining at the leash. 'And you shut your mouth, Benteen.'

'Or?' the narrowed-lipped Texan snarled.

'Ain't doing no good fighting among ourselves,' Bull Rankin wisely counselled.

Cy Brodie walked off a distance to hide the worry that clouded his brown eyes, his hands fretting his dark hair. After a moment, Bull Rankin strolled over to join him. Matter-of-factly, he said, 'Gabby's had it, Cy. You know that.'

'That old man's as tough as bullhide,' Brodie countered.

'Not tough enough to make it across the border, I reckon. There's even harder country ahead than we've been over.'

Rankin let time slip by before he spoke again. Cy Brodie knew what was coming.

'We'll have to leave the old man behind, Cy.' Rankin was talking sound sense. 'Gabby's been on the owlhoot trail long enough to know that this is the way it's got to be.'

Cy hated the idea of leaving Gabby Scanell to die alone.

'You know it's the only thing to do, Cy,' Rankin said. 'Want me to tell him?'

Brodie came to a decision. 'You and the boys head out. I'll stay with Gabby.'

Rankin's jaw dropped. 'That's pure loco.'

'I owe Gabby, Bull.'

Brodie's mind drifted back two years to a card game in a one-horse town in Utah. He could still feel the freezing cold of the snowstorm that had driven them into Skewer Bend for shelter. The saloon was a warm and cheap place to while away the hours until the blizzard passed.

'Like to fall in?' the man dealing poker invited Cy.

Not having the poke to join in, Cy had at first refused the man's invitation. However, Gabby Scanell had reckoned that if the rest were to pool their resources and stake Cy, being such a sharp poker player, their investment would be repaid with a healthy profit.

That was how he got into the game. Soon the bills and coin in front of him began to pile up until, soured, the men around the table began to question Cy Brodie's luck. Seeing what was coming, Cy tried to pull out of the game but no one would wear that.

'You gotta chunk of our money, mister,' the man who had invited Cy to join the game growled. 'It's only proper me and the boys here be given a chance to haul it back.'

Cy Brodie had asked quietly, 'What if I don't lose?'

A hawkish man who was halfway down his second bottle of whiskey slurred, 'You can't keep winnin' for ever.'

'Except...'

Another man left his unfinished accusation hang in the air. But no one had any trouble in filling in the blank spaces.

Cy said, 'My game is fair.'

'You say?' his accuser barked. 'But luck like yours don't often come 'round, mister.'

Brodie asked grimly, 'Are you saying that I'm dealing dirty?'

A wave of unease swept round the table. Brodie's accuser looked to his fellow towns-men for backing, but eyes were shifting away from him faster that a snake's spit. Abandoned, and faced with what would be the inevitable result of unequivocally stating what he thought, the big-bellied man backed off.

'All I'm sayin', mister, is that I wish the cards liked me as much as they do you.'

'I'm not sure that that doesn't mean the same thing, dolled up,' Brodie had pressed, irked by the man's accusation.

'Sandy's got a mouth that most times is best kept shut,' said a prune-faced man who had not spoken before, his dead-fish eyes shifting to Cy's partners bellied up to the bar. 'Let's play cards.'

'I'd prefer to call it quits now,' Cy Brodie said. He shoved half the pile in front of him to the centre of the table. 'Just let's say that I'm buying myself out, gents.'

'Your choice,' the man who had invited him into the game said, grateful for the kickback with only lining left in his pockets. 'Boys, say thanks to the stranger.'

Mumbled thanks drifted round the table. Clearly, it was a halfway house settlement for most. But luckily no one's anger had become fired up enough to challenge Cy Brodie, and, not a man given to killing if it could be avoided, he was grateful for that.

But there were two kinds of anger: the flashing kind, and the smouldering kind. It was the latter which had almost put paid to Cy Brodie an hour later when he went to relieve himself in the saloon's privy out back. The man who had invited him into the game had got greedy. It was Gabby Scanell, lurking in the shadows close to the privy, who had saved Cy from the flashing knife in the man's hand.

Gabby dispatched him with a shotgun – both barrels.

That's why Cy Brodie owed Gabby Scanell big time.

'You and the boys hit the trail,' Brodie told Bull Rankin. 'Gabby and me will follow in a couple of days. We'll meet up at the roost.'

'Don't talk nonsense,' Rankin said. 'Gabby Scanell is done for. He's got a slug in his gut. It's a mystery how he's lasted this long.' He warned, 'Stay 'round here and that posse is likely to drop by and string you up from the nearest tree.'

'I was thinking that if Gabby could reach Bowen Crossing...' Cy ruminated.

Rankin yelped. 'Bowen Crossing? That's Bob Latchford's town, Cy. Latchford is the toughest lawman in these parts. He'll likely kill you on sight, or at best toss you in jail.'

21

Rankin looked beyond Brodie to the smoke rising from the hills.

'And are you forgetting about the Apaches?'

'I'm not that much of a fool, Bull,' Cy said tersely.

'Then show it, man,' Rankin growled. 'Even if you manage to dodge the posse, and the Indians, Latchford will nail you. Those are odds only a fool would take.'

'I owe Gabby, Bull,' Cy said uncompromisingly. 'He saved my life.'

'You paid him back a hundred times over by keeping him on, when all sense said he should have been put out to grass.'

Cy Brodie stated emphatically, 'This toing and froing is over with, Bull. The debt to Gabby is mine to repay, and mine alone. Now I'd appreciate if you fellas got out of my hair and let me make plans.'

'Is that your final say?'

'It is, Bull.'

'Let's ride, Rankin.'

They swung around to find Jack Benteen behind them, ears cocked. Brodie reacted angrily.

'Don't like creepers, Benteen.'

'Creeper?' the Texan snarled. His hand hovered over his pistol. 'Ain't never been called that before. Don't like bein' called it now neither.'

Cy Brodie squared up. Bull Rankin stepped between them.

'I don't give a damn who kills who,' he glowered 'but a gunshot will bring all sorts of ornery critters crawling over these rocks, and that puts my hide at risk.' He grabbed the rifle from his saddle scabbard and levelled it at both men, warning, 'If either of you draw iron, he's going to pay the full damn price for his foolishness!'

Bull Rankin was a strange mixture. Fiercely loyal, while at the same time a man who, when threatened, gave no quarter to any man. Now he showed fully that mix of loyalty and self-protective grit.

Jack Benteen dropped his challenge, and declared, 'If anyone wants to join me, I'm hittin' the trail.'

The gang vaulted into their saddles.

Bull Rankin said, 'You make fast tracks for the roost the second Gabby's eyes close, Cy.'

'I will,' Brodie promised.

Cy Brodie watched the gang's dust as they headed through the narrow canyon. Gabby Scanell urged him, 'Leave me be, Cy. My time ain't long.'

Fresh blood merged with the rusty dried blood of an hour before to form an ugly blotch on Gabby's shirt. Flies buzzed busily. Angrily and hopelessly, Cy Brodie swiped at the flies with his Stetson.

Gabby said sombrely, 'Leave 'em be, Cy. They'll have all of me shortly anyway.' His grey, pain-filled eyes glinted angrily. 'And you too, if you don't git right now!'

Cy chanted, 'When're you going to get it through that dumb head of yours that I'm not going anywhere, Gabby. Leastways, not without you in tow.'

Gabby Scanell shook his head. 'You're a darn fool, Cy Brodie. An old man like me has had his time. But you've got good years ahead of you, and you're throwing them all away.'

Mist clouded the old man's eyes. He sighed sadly, and said passionately, 'Shuck the outlaw trail, Cy. Make good on that ranch you've been gabbin' 'bout until my head hurt.'

Gabby Scanell's breathing sounded like a holed bellows. His face had shadows that weren't there an hour before. Grey hollows had formed under his cheekbones. His eyes were looking, yet not seeing, the way a man does when the need to worry about the here and now no longer matters.

On hearing a scrape on a boulder behind him, Brodie swung around, six-gun flashing. A pair of vultures had taken up watch, their greedy eyes on Gabby. Repulsed and angered by the ugly creatures, Brodie instinctively shot them. The boom of the .45 rolled like thunder though the canyon and out across the barren country beyond.

Gabby said, 'That was a damn fool thing to do, Cy.'

Brodie smothered his angst at the old man's criticism, because he knew in his heart the correctness of it. The sound of the gunshot would travel miles. His worry was not about the posse, if they were still in pursuit. The desert played tricks with sound. Unless they had an expert tracker, the gunfire could have come from a hundred different directions. But that would not be the case with the Apache. If the gunfire reached their ears, they would track it unerringly.

'You ain't got no choice now,' Gabby Scanell said. 'You gotta ride like the darn wind, if you want to hold on to that purty hair of yours. Give me my rifle and git while ya can.'

He grinned.

'And if you've got any sense, you'll drop

by Bowen Crossing and grab that gal Kate.'

'Kate?' Cy Brodie asked in surprise.

'That's her name, ain't it? The woman you're in love with. At least that's what it sounded like to me.'

He explained.

'Heard you talk in your sleep a hundred times 'bout her.' His grin widened. 'Sounds too like a mighty fine and elegant woman to me, for a man to waste his time robbin' nickels from banks and riskin' bein' gunshot. Now hand me that damn rifle!'

Brodie thought that he had put Kate Trent out of his mind a long time ago. It surprised him to discover that he had not.

'Call the first babby after me,' Gabby said. 'If it ain't a gal, that is.'

Humouring the old man, Cy said, 'If it's a girl we'll call her Gabrielle.'

'Gabrielle? What kinda damn name is that? Don't sound American to me.'

'It's French, I think.'

'French?' Gabby Scanell's eyes lit up with fond memories. 'Had me a spell with a French woman down New Orleans way once. Her name was,' he sighed, and said her name dreamily, 'Claudette. Asked me to stay with her, too.'

Gabby Scanell's eyes drifted over the arid

canyon, full of the sadness of past mistakes.

'Should have,' he said softly. Drifting deeper into reverie, he continued, 'Claudette had this four-poster bed, soft as her touch. Always planned that when my time came, it would be in such a rig that I'd breathe my last.'

He sighed with Good Friday hopelessness. 'Guess that ain't going to happen now.'

Prompted by Gabby Scanell's reminiscing, Kate Trent came back to haunt Cy Brodie. His vision of her was of that very first time he saw her at Sullivan's Creek on the Crichton range, when he was roping a rogue steer. Sight of her had sucked the breath from him and made his head spin. A mane of red hair, and eyes as green as spring grass.

And he could see Kate sashaying along the boardwalk in town, every male eye rivetted to her, always on the verge of mischief.

Sundays, Kate was Ned Crichton's dinner guest. The old bull was hopeful that Kate would look kindly on his son Jody.

'Kate has the hips to fill this range with kids,' he had been overheard saying to Jody. And he urged him to waste no time in making Kate his. 'Before she takes up with Cy Brodie. I've seen the way she looks at him, and the breathless way he watches her,

27

boy,' he had warned his heir. 'Better move fast.'

There weren't many truly eligible women in Bowen Crossing for the rancher's son to marry. And fewer still beautiful ones.

When Kate would arrive at the ranch every man's heart would beat faster, and none faster than Cy Brodie's.

'Kate will have nothing to do with Jody Crichton,' Bob Latchford would predict each and every Sunday. 'He ain't man enough to tame a woman of Kate Trent's spirit.'

'Is there a man in these parts who could?' Cy would ponder.

'Sure is,' Latchford would say. Sticking out his chest, he'd declare, 'Me!'

Cy never made his views known, and never got involved in bunkhouse banter about how Kate might be tamed. His thoughts then were as secret as the thoughts he harboured in the quiet hours of the night when thinking about Kate made sleep impossible. He had a notion that Kate looked at him in a way she did not look at the others, including Jody Crichton.

His notion was confirmed as fact when, trembling like the last fall leaf, Cy asked Kate to the Harvest Ball, (a fancy handle for a barn dance, because the Crichtons and other big ranchers gave the modest dance their patronage) and she had said with that impish grin of hers, 'I'd surely be delighted to accept your invitation, Cy.'

Cy Brodie had thought that his happiness would blow the top of his head right off. But his joy was fleeting.

'Pack your traps and get out, Brodie,' was Ned Crichton's angry reaction.

On hearing the news of Cy's dismissal, Kate Trent immediately changed her mind about going to the Harvest Ball with him.

'Where do you think you'll get a job in this territory?' she had said. 'Ned Crichton will make his displeasure known to any man who thinks about giving you a job, Cy.'

'I don't care,' Cy had said defiantly. 'Let him.'

But Kate, though her heart was breaking, took back her acceptance of his invitation and made it known that should Ned Crichton withdraw Cy Brodie's dismissal, she would accompany Jody Crichton to the Harvest Ball.

It happened that way. But Ned Crichton's poison towards Cy was not done with. Brodie was a thorn in his side, so he thought up a scheme to rid the territory of Cy Brodie for good.

The rancher handed Cy the task of delivering a prize bull to a friend at the other end of the county. Brodie, being a scrupulously honest man himself, did not suspect any connivery on Ned Crichton's part. The rancher's deviousness only came home when, halfway through his journey, a posse descended on him and arrested him for rustling. There was a trial. Ned Crichton flatly denied that Cy was on his errand. The jury, all too eager to stay in Crichton's good books, returned a verdict of guilty without deliberation, the second the judge's gavel closed the proceedings.

He faced twenty years breaking rocks.

Ned Crichton had cleverly removed the obstacle to Kate Trent marrying his son. However, good fortune smiled on Cy Brodie.

The celebrations which followed the verdict made a drunk deputy careless, and he left the key in the cell door before passing out. Cy rode hell for leather. But despite his good fortune, Cy reckoned that he had ridden away from Bowen Crossing, the poorer man for having to leave Kate Trent behind. Gabby Scanell cut in on Cy's reverie.

'Goin' to give me that rifle or not?'

'Sure, I'll give you your rifle, Gabby,' Cy said.

'At last you're gettin' sense,' Gabby crowed. But in his eyes there was a hint of disappointment. 'If I'm still sucking air when whoever heard that gunshot shows up, I'll do my best to buy you time, Cy,' he promised.

'You do that, Gabby,' Brodie said.

Cy vaulted urgently into the saddle, and set off at as fast a pace as the canyon terrain would allow.

'Might have said goodbye,' Gabby Scanell said, once the clatter of Cy Brodie's departure faded.

A deadly stillness crept along the canyon. Gabby looked to the canyon's high walls, and to the vultures dotting the rocks and boulders, their greedy black eyes watching him weaken, patiently savouring the feast to come. Gabby, like all Westerners, hated buzzards. It had always been his fear that one day they would feed on him.

And now his fear was about to come to pass.

'Guess that dyin' in that fancy four-poster, ain't goin' to happen now,' Gabby Scanell murmured.

# CHAPTER THREE

Cy Brodie saw sign of unshod ponies near the creek he was headed for. Indians. He dismounted and hid his horse in a hollow. He then gathered some tumbleweed and tossed it about at the entrance to the hollow, careful to make it look like a natural formation of undergrowth, while at the same time hiding the entrance as best he could. The ruse would not fool the Apaches. But it might very well trick the posse.

A while earlier, he had spotted a wispy dust cloud which he reckoned was not raised by the Indians, only a handful of riders was responsible for it. The posse had started out with twelve men. A later sighting had been of about half that number. And on a later sighting still, Cy had counted only four riders.

As with all posses, enthusiasm had waned and men dropped out. With Indians on the prowl, it showed that the men who had stuck with the pursuit were dogged in their determination to snare the Brodie gang. It was a determination which Cy Brodie found hard to understand, considering the small pickings the gang had made.

The task of hiding his horse completed, Cy made his way the last half-mile to the creek on legs with a feather-light touch, carefully picking each step so as not to dislodge shale or displace a rock that would alert anyone to his presence. Along with the posse and the Indians, there was also the chance of crossing paths with men who, like himself, had no desire to meet strangers.

The border country was home to a host of desperadoes in transit to and from Mexico; men who did not have Cy Brodie's qualms about killing.

Cy had expected the posse's indignation to cool, that they would abandon the chase. But it had not happened. His knowledge of the country's canyons, ravines and gullies had helped him in shaking off the Gila Junction posse, but in doing so, he had lost sight of them and was now disadvantaged by not knowing where they might pop up.

Brodie safely reached the willow-shaded creek he was aiming for, but it took a whole lot longer than he had planned. His worry was for Gabby Scanell. The sun was slipping low on the horizon, but it still had plenty of heat in it to sap a healthy man's energy, let alone a man in Gabby's weakened condition.

He took comfort from the fact that there had been no shooting, which meant, he hoped, that the posse, Apaches, or any of the other predators roaming the desert country had not come upon Gabby. Stemming his eagerness to hurry down the shale trail to the creek proved wise when, from out of a gully at the far end of the creek two Indians emerged – scouts Brodie reckoned. They were chattering excitedly. From the little Apache lingo Cy understood, he gathered that they were arguing about which direction to take.

The older warrior was pointing correctly to the south of the creek in the direction where Gabby Scanell was. The young buck wanted to head north of the creek, away from the canyon where Gabby was. All Cy Brodie could do was await the outcome of the argument. If the older warrior won out, he'd be faced with taking action to save Gabby Scanell's hide. But in so doing, there was every chance he could lose his own life.

Brodie looked anxiously to the dipping sun. Shadows were creeping across the creek, deepening by the minute. If the dispute between the Apaches went on much longer it would be dusk and they would probably return to their camp, because of the Apaches' fear of the dark.

The argument did not last.

'We go my way,' the older warrior ordered the younger buck.

Once the older man had spoken, the buck accepted his decision, handing Cy Brodie a dilemma he could have done without. He edged back into the shadows, becoming a shadow himself. He slid the Bowie from its sheath on his gunbelt. A sudden breeze disturbed the branches of a willow near Cy, letting through a shaft of light from the dying sun that flashed on the shining steel of the hunting knife. Cy held his breath. Had the Indians seen the diamond-bright flash?

As the seconds ticked by and the Apaches kept riding at an amble along the creek towards the exit at the south end, passing directly beneath Brodie, Cy began to breathe a little easier, but only just a little easier. There was no guarantee that the Indians had not seen the flash from the Bowie blade. He knew Apaches, and knew their swiftness of thought and their ability to hide surprise.

'Sun go,' the buck said. 'We go, too.'

The older warrior drew rein to look about him at the quickly fading light.

'Not far,' he told his partner. 'We go.'

Cy Brodie's rising hope was dashed. He readied himself to spring on the Indians. His only chance was to kill one quickly, and hope that surprise slowed the other's reaction the couple of seconds he would need to have a chance of a fight on equal terms with the second Indian. But which one first? The young buck obviously would be the preferred one. But then that would leave the wilier of the two to contend with, and in Cy Brodie's experience, wile often won out over brawn.

On they came, changing sides all the time, their meandering progress giving Cy no chance to pick his target. He had ridden his luck of late. He wondered now how much luck he had left?

A few more seconds and he would find out.

## CHAPTER FOUR

Bob Latchford looked up from the monthly report he was writing for the town council when four men piled into his office, the dust of the desert on their clothing and etched in the lines of their faces. The impromptu interruption annoyed the Bowen Crossing marshal. His writing skills were not great, and any break in his concentration set him back, making it necessary for him to focus anew when he resumed penning his report.

Latchford figured that he was looking at the Gila Junction posse. He was not impressed. The leader of the group of four had the soft hands and skin of a man whose work would ill prepare him for the arduous task of riding with a posse. The other men, too, in age and demeanour were as equally out of place.

The newfangled telegraph had alerted Latchford about the robbery at the Gila Junction bank. But more troubling was the news of who the perpetrators were – the Brodie gang. The last man Bob Latchford wanted anyway near Bowen Crossing at the best of times was Cy Brodie, but the day before his wedding it came perilously close to outright disaster.

'Marshal Latchford,' the posse leader boomed. 'Greetings, sir. The name's Ethan Briscoe. President of the Gila Junction Bank.'

Latchford slid his eyes back to the report he was struggling with, telling his visitors without directly saying so, that their intrusion was unwelcome.

Briscoe was not fazed.

'We, Marshal,' – the bank president's hand waved over the men with him – 'are the Gila Junction posse. In hot pursuit of the Brodie gang.'

Briscoe made the announcement with all the ceremony and pomposity of a man not used to contradiction or argument.

'Kind of a small posse, ain't it?' Latchford observed drily.

'We were twelve, Marshal. The others did not have the grit to stay the course.'

'Why a posse at all?' the Bowen Crossing marshal enquired. 'Story is that the Brodie gang got away with only a fistful of dollars. Not worth saddling up to retrieve.'

Briscoe thundered, 'It isn't the amount of money stolen, Marshal Latchford. Thieving is thieving, and should be discouraged by harsh measures and penalties.' The bank president said, critically, 'Surely, as a lawman you would be of the same view, sir?'

'Gila Junction business is no business of mine,' Latchford declared.

'Clearly, Marshal Latchford,' Briscoe intoned, 'we need more men. I'm requesting that you use the authority of your office to help me acquire them.'

'Sheriff Haskell is your law,' Latchford growled.

Ethan Briscoe threw his hands in the air. 'Sheriff Haskell hasn't sobered up for the last month.'

'Hah!' a smallish man behind Briscoe scoffed. 'Most of a year, Ethan.' Fiery eyes set in a wizened face bore into Bob Latchford. 'A mite uncooperative ain't ya, Marshal?'

'Oh, don't take umbrage so, Larry,' the banker scolded. 'I'm sure Marshal Latchford is a mighty busy fella. A man has a lot to do on the eve of his wedding.'

Ethan Briscoe's knowledge showed him to be a careful and cautious man, having done his homework before his visit.

'You got that right,' Latchford growled.

Ethan Briscoe let the silence drag for a spell, before continuing, 'I hear that Cy Brodie is from around these parts, Marshal?'

'He is,' Latchford replied brusquely.

'Friend of yours?' the smallish man asked.

'Folk might reckon that way,' Latchford conceded.

Briscoe said, 'One of the gang, an old-timer, caught lead. Must be in pretty bad shape...'

'Bad enough for Cy Brodie to seek the help of an old friend,' a lanky man who had

39

hung back said.

Latchford's retort was needle sharp. 'Cy Brodie is a wanted man in this town. If he shows he'll have to pay the full price for his wrongdoing.'

'I admire your steel, Marshal,' Briscoe said. 'But I figure that instead of waiting around for Brodie to show, if he'll show, you should be actively seeking him out.'

Latchford glared at the banker.

'You'd say?' he growled.

'I'd say,' the Gila Junction banker stated unequivocally.

The marshal said, grumpily, 'You want Brodie, Mr Briscoe, you go find him. Like I said, Gila Junction business is Gila Junction business, and none of mine. If Brodie puts in an appearance, I'll nail him. But I'm not going looking for him.'

Bob Latchford had appreciated Cy Brodie giving Bowen Crossing a wide berth since he had busted out of the town jail two years previously, and he hoped that he would never lay eyes on his old saddle partner while he wore a star, because it would give him no pleasure at all to see Cy Brodie breaking rocks.

The marshal had often pondered on the twist of fate that had forced Cy Brodie into outlawry. Cy was not a liar or a thief. Ned Crichton, on the other hand, was a tough-as-nails *hombre* used to getting his own way, and would not balk at treachery to get what he wanted. That his plans to have Kate Trent become Mrs Jody Crichton had been thwarted would not have settled well with him.

Both men had axes to grind. Ned Crichton might have railroaded Brodie. On the other hand, Cy might have seen Ned Crichton's prize bull as compensation for his unfair treatment. Whatever the ins and outs of the affair, as a lawman he would have to respect the verdict of the court which put Cy Brodie squarely in the wrong, if he showed his face in Bowen Crossing.

Huffily, Ethan Briscoe enquired of Latchford, 'Have you got any objections to my raising a posse without your blessing, Marshal?'

The marshal shrugged. 'What you do with your dollars is your business, Mr Briscoe.'

'Would you deputize such men?' the banker asked.

'Nope,' came the blunt reply. 'You hire: you're responsible.'

Stung, Briscoe retorted haughtily, 'I must warn you, Marshal Latchford, that I intend to take up your grudging approach with some lofty friends of mine.'

Latchford growled, 'The last man who threatened me, Briscoe, nursed a broken jaw.'

Irked by Latchford's abrasive response, the bank president flung back, 'Might your reluctance to help be motivated by your friendship with–'

Before Briscoe could take a step back, Latchford reached across his desk and grabbed a fistful of the banker's shirt.

'I sport an honest badge, Briscoe,' he flared. 'Any man who says I don't risks being planted. Now get out!' Latchford dropped Briscoe back on his heels. 'Seems to me, that by now, Cy Brodie will be clear across the border anyway and out of US jurisdiction.'

Briscoe snorted. 'The Mex border doesn't pose a problem for us, Marshal Latchford.'

The lawman glared flintily at the posse leader.

'I figure, mister, that if we demand that the Mexicans keep to their side of the Rio Grande, then we're honour bound to do the same.'

'You favour letting every no-good rest on his laurels in Mexico?' Briscoe challenged.

'They all come back, eventually.'

Briscoe rattled off, 'We're not prepared to

wait that long!'

Bob Latchford cast the banker a curious look.

'Exactly how much did the Brodie gang heist?' he asked.

Briscoe became instantly evasive.

'How much could the Gila Junction Bank hold?' Latchford wondered. 'Last time I was in Gila Junction, it didn't impress me as being a very prosperous place. In fact, most of it was barely standing, as I recall.'

Briscoe railed, 'Like I said, Marshal, the amount doesn't matter. Robbery is robbery, plain and simple.'

Latchford's curiosity became keener. 'Unusual for a banker to chase his own dollars, ain't it? Kind of duddily dressed for a manhunt. Never saw a posseman before who wore a silk waistcoat.'

Ethan Briscoe shuffled his feet and averted his gaze from Latchford's to a point beyond the marshal.

'So, tell me, Briscoe,' Latchford persisted, 'how much did Brodie heist?'

Briscoe mumbled, 'A couple of hundred dollars.'

Astounded, Bob Latchford asked, 'You're willing to risk your neck with Apaches on the prowl for a couple of hundred dollars.'

'Like I said—'

'I know, it's not the amount but the principle,' the marshal finished. 'Now,' – Latchford returned his attention to the report he was writing – 'I've got a report to finish and a wedding to prepare for, gents.'

'Good day, Marshal,' the Gila Junction banker barked. He swept out of the law office with his cronies on his coat tail.

Latchford forgot the report he was writing. His face set in grim lines. Sometimes, like right now, he wished he had never pinned on a star. He had still been nursing cows on Crichton range when Cy Brodie busted out of jail, and maybe that's where he should have stayed. He had only put on a badge when the former marshal, Dan McCauley, had bought a knife in the gut when he had arrested a drunk, and had let the drunk's age fool him in to thinking that the oldster was beyond malice.

Latchford's frown deepened. Cy Brodie must have criss-crossed the border time and time again and had never visited. Why should he now? He would surely know the consequences if he showed. The marshal was sure that he was fretting over nothing. But no matter how many times he told himself so, he could not shake the feeling of trouble heading his way.

With Cy Brodie out of the picture and nursing a common grief, Kate Trent and he had become close. In Brodie's place, how would he react if his former best friend had stolen his girl and was about to toss him back in jail?

Mighty angrily, was Bob Latchford's conclusion.

## CHAPTER FIVE

Cy Brodie tensed his leg muscles to launch himself at the Apache just below him in the creek. The younger buck, still sulking, had allowed a gap to open up between him and the older Apache which, Cy hoped, would give him the time to slash the elder's throat and throw the hunting knife at the younger. Brodie was not a knife-loving man, preferring a pistol, but he was grateful now that he had taken the lessons which Bull Rankin had persuaded him to take a couple of months previously during a hiatus in an Arizona hideout. He hoped that he had been an attentive student and had learned well. The next few seconds would tell.

Cy sprang from hiding. The older Apache looked up as Brodie dropped in free fall from the boulder above him, his every second occupied with what he would do if the Apache's reactions were fast. The Indian could simply veer his horse a foot or two, and Cy would crash on to the cushionless stony creek-bed covered only by a trickle of water. Bones would likely break if that happened, and he would be at the Apaches' mercy, which would be no mercy at all.

Another blood-chilling prospect was that the Apache's reactions would be swift enough for him to get his knife free of its sheath and wait for Cy to plunge on to it. The third possibility, and equally as horrendous, was that the younger Indian would simply use the rifle he was carrying across his lap.

All in all, as he dropped, Cy Brodie was trying to find a reason for the loco chance he was taking.

He could have followed the Apaches and waited to spring his trap if they got too close to Gabby Scanell. Maybe Gabby wasn't even alive to begin with?

His action could be a fool's folly, for which he could pay a terrible price.

In the harsh country he was in, Cy Brodie

knew that kindness, compassion and loyalty were often the undoing of a man when, all round him, there were other men bereft of such fine feelings, their own survival at all cost their sole objective.

The Indian grabbed for his knife. Its wicked blade flashed. Cy Brodie's heart skittered. The outlaw jerked his body in an attempt to speed up his descent. It worked. But would it be enough? If the Apache got the blade pointed upwards...

# CHAPTER SIX

Bob Latchford came to the law office door to look after Ethan Briscoe and his partners. They turned into the saloon where, for a bottle of rotgut and a couple of dollars, the banker would find the men he needed among the town's dregs. They would not be of the calibre of men who should ideally form a posse. But then, Latchford reckoned that the banker was not interested in the quality of the posse, only in its deadliness. The marshal had no doubt that if they snared Cy Brodie, hanging tree justice would be his lot.

It was a real puzzler to Latchford why a banker, even a robbed banker, was heading up a posse. Men who spent their days lifting nothing heavier than their butt from a plush chair seldom, if ever, put that butt in a hot saddle, and took the risk of riding into the lawless territory of New Mexico. They got other, less fortunate men, to do that for them.

But was Ethan Briscoe a typical banker? He looked and dressed the part, but something lurking below the gloss of his fine duds and smooth face was out of kilter with his outward veneer of respectability.

A wise *hombre* once said that the eyes were the windows of the soul. If that was true, there was a canker of rottenness inside Ethan Briscoe.

Cy Brodie was on the Apache's back, his knife slashing the Indian's throat. Blood, hot and sticky, ran up his sleeve. The smell of the Apache's last meal wafted sickeningly out of the opened throat. Though fatally wounded, the Indian used the last of his strength to hook an arm around Brodie's head. The Apache's hold could not last very long, but the headlock would give the other Indian the chance to regain his wits and act.

48

The Apache toppled from his pony. Luck deserted Cy as he crashed into the creek pinned under the Indian. The impact on the rocky creek-bed sent numbing pain shooting along his every nerve. He reckoned that his luck had finally run out, as all luck must. The dead Indian was at least thirty pounds heavier than he was, and shifting him would take more time than he had. But luck, being a fickle lady, changed her mind again when the dead Apache's body shielded him from the younger Indian's rifle bullets.

Brodie had lost his gun in the fall. It now lay tantalizingly close, but just out of reach. Cy grabbed a stick and tried to scoop the Colt towards him, but the rotten stick cracked and the pistol fell back, bounced off a rock, and landed up even further away.

Brodie was helpless; the Apache dismounted, his grin cruel. Keeping the outlaw under threat of his rifle, he came to stand over Cy. He was in no hurry. His attacker was vanquished. The white man's death would be slow and as painful as he could make it.

The Indian set his rifle aside and drew his knife. Cy Brodie shook. An Apache could kill a man very slowly with a knife, peeling away layer after layer of skin and flesh until his victim begged for death. The buck confirmed his intentions.

'White man, you die the Apache way.'

Cy Brodie had lost.


# CHAPTER SEVEN

Gabby Scanell wondered how he was still alive. The burning in his gut had the fury of hellfire. His vision blurred. The canyon filled with threatening shadows. What was real? What was imaginary? Rustlings. Snarling. The scraping of vultures' claws.

Helpless.

Terrified.

Gabby turned his mind to times past to chase away his fears; the women, the cards, the booze, and the very elegant Claudette Simone. His memories were sweet. Bitter. Passionate. A couple of times, when the fever scattered his senses, he saw Claudette standing right in front of him, smiling that luring, crooked smile of hers that turned men to jelly.

And he remembered that handsome four-poster in which they had romped. No way now that he was going to meet his Maker from such a fancy rig. But he reckoned the odds against that ever happening had been stacked against him from the cradle.

Gabby had tried hard work and honest living. He had ridden shotgun on a Fargo stage. Hauled freight. Tried prospecting. He had even worn, with no small amount of pride, a deputy's star. He reckoned that putting on that star had put him where he was now, all shot up and a meal for the critters gathering in the canyon.

He could still hear the nighttime jangle of the saloon piano in Bounty Bend, Wyoming – a town as raw as fresh steak, with more mud than gold; more hope than promise; more sin than goodness. Bounty Bend had sprung up on the promise of a palm-sized nugget found in a mountain stream. The hardware store and the saloon were the busiest places in town. Shovels and picks sailed out the hardware door by day, and the saloon drowned the prospectors' sorrows by night. In those two businesses there was real gold. When Bounty Bend folded, the owners of those two establishments left with full pockets, moving on to the next town living on a promise of riches.

On his last night in what had become a ghost town, Gabby had peered through a lighted window at Charles Tanner, the town shyster, who had shrewdly invested in the hardware store and the saloon and had amassed a fortune, most of which he kept under the floorboards of his sitting-room, making only token deposits in the town bank to avert attention from the real pile secreted in his house.

Deputy Gabby Scanell could have turned left instead of right that night, as he had done on his rounds each night for over a year, but he had not. Why? It was a question he had often asked himself over the years. Cruel fate at its meanest, he reckoned. Seeing Tanner with thick rolls of dollar bills in his mitts triggered a larcenous streak in Gabby.

Bounty Bend was finished. He'd be moving on. Where to, Lord only knew. He had worked hard over the years, and had only a couple of hundred dollars to show for it. Honesty had not proved to be very lucrative. And right there, in Charles Tanner's hands, there was more money than Gabby would earn in ten lifetimes of honest labour.

It was a temptation too much to resist.

Gabby Scanell slipped around the back, prised open the kitchen window and crept inside. He waited in the dark hallway until Tanner came from the sitting-room and

52

waylaid him. The gun barrel which Gabby laid across the lawyer's head should have been enough to poleaxe him. But apparently lawyers' heads were as thick as their hides, and the blow only stunned Tanner. Gabby had left Bounty Bend helter-skelter. A month later, he saw a wanted poster with his dial on it. From there on, and he supposed from the very second he had decided to rob Tanner, he was headed for an outlaw's life.

'Now you ain't got nothin' to whine 'bout when them critters will tear you 'part, you old fool,' he told himself.

If he had had sense and put the take from his thieving to productive use, once the furore died down, he might be lying in that four-poster fit for an English lord right now, with soft feathers under his head instead of rocks.

'A man gets cards,' Gabby Scanell murmured weakly. 'How he plays the hand is up to him.' A vulture pecked at his leg. Gabby opened a weepy eye. 'Git, bird!' he said. 'Ain't time yet.'

Cy Brodie heard a *whoosh* go past him. He saw the glint of a blade. The Indian gagged, clutching at the knife in his throat. Bull Rankin emerged from the willows and took the knife from the dead Apache's throat. He wiped it clean on his sleeve.

'Can't I leave you alone for a second, Cy Brodie,' he said, 'without you getting into all kinds of trouble?'

Cy let out a long sigh of relief. 'Thought you'd be across the border by now, Bull?'

'Figured I would be too,' he said shortly.

'I owe you, Bull,' Cy said.

Rankin shrugged. 'What the hell're you doing here, Cy? Off the beaten track for the border trail, ain't you?'

'I'm not headed for the border yet.'

'Gabby still sucking air?'

'Was the last time I saw him.' Cy explained, 'I came here to cut some willow branches to make a sled.'

'A sled? What for?'

'To haul Gabby to Bowen Crossing. Don't figure he could stay in the saddle.'

Astonished, Bull Rankin yelped, 'Bowen Crossing?'

Cy Brodie reasoned, 'Gabby might have a chance of making it to Bowen Crossing. But he sure as hell wouldn't make it to Mexico.'

'He won't make it no matter what you do, Cy. You're wasting time and likely putting your neck in a noose into the bargain.'

'It's my neck, Bull,' Cy Brodie answered quietly.

Bull Rankin nodded. 'That it is. I guess I've wasted my time riding back here to talk sense into that skull of yours?'

'There's a heck of a fine sawbones in Bowen Crossing; Doc Hockley. I've seen him work miracles...'

Rankin snorted. 'That's what Gabby'll need sure enough.'

'If I can get Gabby to Hockley, he'll stand a chance.'

'And what about Latchford?' Bull Rankin quizzed, and warned, 'He ain't going to turn a blind eye to your presence, Cy.'

'I'm figuring on being long gone before anyone knows I've been, Bull.'

'And just how do you figure on doing that?'

'By dropping Gabby on Hockley's doorstep while it's still dark.'

Bull Rankin's astonishment before, was nothing compared to his bewilderment now.

'That would mean–'

'Getting Gabby off this mountain during the night,' Cy said.

Rankin declared, 'It's likely you'll fall right off this damn rock if you try!'

'Maybe. But I've got to try, Bull,' he said with grim finality.

'And if Latchford nails you?'

'I guess I'll be on my way to breaking rocks for most of my natural,' Cy said sombrely.

Bull Rankin held Brodie's gaze. 'You know,' he said, 'you're not cut out for this kind of life, Cy. When you ride on, if you ride on, I reckon you should keep on going until you get to nursing those cows you've been dreaming of.'

Cy Brodie said, angrily, 'Having my own ranch is just that, Bull. A damn dream!'

'Others have turned their backs on outlawry and made a go of it,' Rankin reminded him. 'You could be one of those men, 'cause you ain't an outlaw by nature. If you were you'd be drinking tequila and bedding a Mex whore by now. Not nursemaiding an old man, who at worse is dead, or as good as, and at best has his days numbered.'

'And you, Bull?' Brodie quizzed. 'What're you doing here?'

He snorted. 'Not to nurse Gabby Scanell, that's for sure.' He grinned, bringing a warm relief to normally implacable features. 'I turned tail to get you out of the fix I was sure you'd get yourself into. And I figured right, too.'

'Nursemaiding is nursemaiding, Bull,'

Brodie drawled. 'And I'm damn glad you showed when you did, that I can tell you.'

Bull Rankin growled, 'I came back to talk sense to you, Cy Brodie. And I figure that I wasted good drinking and whoring time by doing so!'

Brodie turned his thoughts to the task which had brought him to the creek.

'Guess I'd best gather the makings of that sled before any other critter puts in an appearance. You head out, Bull,' he counselled. 'Don't see any point in you losing your scalp, or being lynched by the Gila Junction posse on account of my foolishness.'

'Guess that makes sense.' Rankin strode to his horse and mounted up. 'Wish you'd change your mind and head for Mexico, Cy.'

'Save some tequila for me. I'll see you fellas in a couple of days.'

'Want me to reserve that fiery filly Conchita for you?'

'No.'

'You know, Cy,' Bull Rankin said, 'your resistance to women worries me sometimes. Ain't natural for a man to keep his pants on with a woman like Conchita Delgado hot for him.'

Cy Brodie had a secret he had kept from

his fellow outlaws which explained his ability to spurn a fine woman like Conchita Delgado and many more along the trails: he had a woman of his own; a feisty beauty who put all other females in the shade. Her name was Kate Trent. Fool that he was, he had never told Kate how he felt. And he figured that telling her when he had been tossed into jail and facing a life of rock-breaking, was no time at all. Now he'd run out of time and chances. Kate would long since have become Mrs Jody Crichton. Time, he had told himself, would heal his aching heart. But lately he was thinking that there just wasn't enough time made to accomplish that healing.

There were risks for him in taking Gabby Scanell to Bowen Crossing, other than facing Bob Latchford, should it come to that. Anyone in town would gladly snare him. Rustling in cow country was an unforgivable crime, even if it amounted to only one bull. And there was Kate Trent. Bullets were not the only thing that could tear a man's heart apart.

# CHAPTER EIGHT

Kate Trent's excitement was misunderstood by the dressmaker, as she stood the bride-to-be in front of the full-length mirror in Emily Wayne's shop.

'Prettiest bride this town has ever had, I reckon,' Emily genuinely complimented.

Kate ran her hands over the fine satin gown, her eyes filling with tears.

'You like it, don't you?' Emily fretted. 'Finest I've ever made, I'd say.'

'It's lovely, Emily,' Kate said, in a voice constricted by emotion. 'Really beautiful.'

As pleased as a leprechaun sitting at the end of a rainbow, the dressmaker opined, 'I say that it's the woman making the dress, rather than the dress making the woman, Kate.' Then, gently scolding, 'Now shush your crying. What in tarnation have you got to cry about anyway? Every woman in town would switch places with you to have Bob Latchford's boots under her bed. You're a darn lucky girl, Kate. Marshal Latchford is quite a catch.'

'Oh, I know that, Emily,' Kate said. 'Bob is a good and kind man...'

'Heck,' the dressmaker yelped, 'you're not having second thoughts, are you, Kate?' Then, answering her own question, 'Of course you aren't. You're just nervous like every other bride I've togged out.'

'I guess,' Kate said, doubtfully.

Kate Trent's soulful response brought renewed interest from Emily.

'Kate...?'

Having been friends for a long time, ever since they had arrived in town within a couple of days of each other, Kate knew of no one else in whom she would rather confide. She blurted out, 'I'm not sure I want to marry Bob Latchford, Emily.'

'Knock me down with a feather,' Emily Wayne said. 'Have you got brain fever?'

'Maybe I had brain fever to accept Bob's proposal to start with, Emily,' Kate worried. 'When...'

'When what?'

Kate's shoulders slumped. 'When I think I'm in love with another man.'

By now the dressmaker's jaw was down to her navel. 'Another man? Who?'

'Cy Brodie, of course,' Kate wailed.

'Cy Brodie?' Emily exclaimed. 'He's a

convicted man, Kate. Facing at best, when he's caught, imprisonment. And if he's not apprehended, all he's got to offer is a life as an outlaw's woman.'

Emily Wayne shook her head in wonder. 'You'd have to be clean loco to give up a fine man like Bob Latchford for a cur like Cy Bro–'

'Cy is no cur, Emily!' Kate rebuked heatedly.

'Bite my head off if you must,' the dressmaker said. 'But you'd be a fool not to marry Marshal Latchford. Pining for the likes of Cy Brodie. You'll have thrown away your chance at happiness, for sure.'

Casting her mind back, Emily Wayne questioned, 'Besides, you said you *think* you love Cy Brodie? Aren't you sure?'

Miserably, Kate Trent admitted, 'No, Emily. I'm not.'

Emily Wayne was not one of life's natural beauties and had pretty much accepted that spinsterhood was to be her lot. But she had clung to a dream until Bob Latchford had proposed to Kate Trent, of the marshal one day realizing how much she loved and admired him. It had not happened. Emily was the kind of woman men often fled to for comforting, but never for loving.

'Go on,' Emily urged Kate.

'Well, I got this feeling that Cy was about to spill his heart to me just before he set off to deliver Ned Crichton's damn bull. Then, when Cy was wrongly accused and rail-roaded by Crichton, I reckon he kept his thoughts to himself to save me pondering on what might have been for the rest of my days.'

'Pretty fanciful thinking, if you ask me,' was the dressmaker's brusque opinion. 'I think you're just putting obstacles in the way of marrying Bob Latchford.'

'Obstacles? Why would I do that, Emily?'

'Nerves,' the dressmaker pronounced. 'Plain and simple nerves.'

'What have I got to be nervous about? Bob loves me.'

'Of course he does,' Emily reassured her friend. 'Now, you put Cy Brodie clear out of your head, Kate.'

'You're right, Emily. I surely will!'

Being in love with the marshal herself, it had been hard for Emily Wayne to steer Kate so steadfastly in Bob Latchford's direction. The temptation to play on Kate's fears had been difficult to resist, and she had almost succumbed to the old adage of all is fair in love and war. She could take pride in the fact that she had not, but little comfort.

'See you, Bull,' Cy Brodie said.

Bull Rankin rode off aways along the creek before he drew rein. 'I might live to regret this,' he said gruffly. 'I'll help you get Gabby off this darn pile of rock. But I'm going nowhere near Latchford's town. Deal?'

Grinning widely, Cy Brodie said, 'Deal, partner.'

'So, let's get cutting willow to make that sled. I want to be off this mountain and on my way before sun-up.'

Using their hunting knives, Brodie and Rankin soon had enough willow saplings cut to make Gabby Scanell's sled, and were heading back through the moonlit landscape to the canyon where Gabby was. 'Even building an ace sled, Cy,' Rankin said, 'it's going to be one hell of a bumpy ride for Gabby through these canyons and ravines.'

'I'm not planning on using the regular trails, Bull. There's an old prospector's trail that winds close to Bowen Crossing. Pretty steep. But not as bumpy.'

'Old?' Bull Rankin questioned. 'How old? Ain't been a sign of gold in these hills for a long time. No gold, no prospectors. Maybe no trail either, Cy.'

Rankin had brought to the fore the

prospect which Cy Brodie had been avoiding.

'What if that trail has vanished?' Rankin asked. 'Trails don't last long in this country if they're not regularly travelled over.'

'I guess that's a bridge I'll have to cross when I come to it, Bull,' Brodie replied testily. Then, instantly regretting his sharpness of tone which Bull Rankin did not deserve, he apologized. 'Sorry, Bull. There was no call for a sharp tongue.'

'Let's get this done, Cy,' Rankin said.

Ethan Briscoe was standing on the saloon stage when Bob Latchford entered, trying to bring a modicum of calm to the boisterous goings on. For several hours, the banker had kept glasses filled. The end result of his largesse was that every no-good in town and the immediate hinterland had made tracks to the saloon to swill the free booze on offer.

Briscoe had spent handsomely, and now he was about to claim a return on his investment.

Bob Latchford was at a loss to understand why, for the beans and jerky takings from the Gila Junction bank, Ethan Briscoe was willing to add to his losses by providing free liquor and, rumour had it, a hundred dollars a man to ride with him. Briscoe would have a body believe that hunting down Cy Brodie was a matter of principle. However, the marshal reckoned that principle and Briscoe were complete strangers, so that argument flew out the window. That brought Latchford back full circle to *why*?

The marshal hung back at the rear of the saloon to listen to Briscoe's spiel.

'My friends,' he shouted above the babble, 'I need your good and kind assistance...'

'You got it, mister,' a swaying drunk, slugging from a bottle of rotgut cried out. 'Ain't nothin' me an' the boys won't do to help such a decent fella as yourself.'

'Glad to hear it, sir,' the banker called back from the stage.

Briscoe signalled to the barkeep. The drunk's near empty bottle was quickly replaced with a full one. The drunk's coterie added their boozy endorsement to his pledge.

The drunk, Spitter Reilly, a regular visitor to Latchford's cells, demanded silence for Briscoe to be heard and landed a haymaker on a fellow imbiber who ignored his exhortation. The floored man struggled to his feet. He grabbed a bottle from a nearby table, smashed it, and lunged at Reilly.

However, as drunk as the man on whom he was trying to inflict injury, he mistimed his attack. Spitter Reilly kicked his feet from under him. Reilly drew a knife from his boot. He grabbed his attacker by the hair and yanked his head back, exposing his throat ready for the blade.

Latchford's boot shot out to knock the knife from Reilly's grasp. The marshal's fist followed on to land a jaw-breaker that sent Reilly reeling backwards to crash heavily against the stage. The effect of Latchford's intervention was to sober Reilly enough to grab a gun from an onlooker's holster.

Swift as a starving cougar, Latchford sprang at Reilly to smother the threat he posed. The lawman wrenched the pistol from Spitter Reilly's grip and laid the barrel across his face, opening up a deep wound.

The fracas brought a hush to the saloon. Snarling faces surrounded the marshal. The saloon throbbed with danger. Bob Latchford knew that if he showed the slightest sign of weakness, Reilly's drunken friends would be all over him. He grabbed the drunk by the collar, rammed his six-gun in his back and marched him ahead of him through the milling crowd. The batwings seemed a long way off.

'If any man tries anything,' he told the crowd, 'I'll blast Reilly.'

A couple of men who had closed a circle round the marshal moved back as Spitter Reilly's eyes flashed at them.

'A sensible move, fellas,' Latchford said.

Some of the crowd paced Latchford and Reilly, like wild animals waiting for their prey to make a mistake. When they reached the batwings, Latchford warned, 'I'll shoot any man who puts his nose outside the saloon before I lock Reilly up. Understood?'

Glowering faces looked back at him.

As the marshal backed out of the saloon, dragging Spitter Reilly with him, attention was already returning to Ethan Briscoe.

'One hundred dollars each for twelve good men,' the banker announced. 'And,' he added, 'a free bar when we return to town with the Brodie gang.'

'Looks like your friends have other business to attend to, Reilly,' Latchford gloated.

Spitter Reilly shot a killer's look at the marshal.

From inside the saloon Ethan Briscoe was making an announcement which brought a frown to Bob Latchford's face.

'Mr Ike Brown has kindly volunteered to be our leader and guide in this righteous venture to bring Cy Brodie and his cut-throats to the justice they deserve.'

A wild yell of approval exploded from the saloon.

It was Spitter Reilly's turn to gloat.

'Looks like king-sized trouble is brewin', Marshal,' he crowed. 'And you tyin' the knot tomorrow an' all.'

Annoyed, Latchford shoved Reilly ahead of him to the jail. Ike Brown was a gun-fighter in the making. A time or two he had come close to challenging Latchford, but had stayed his hand, not because he had any qualms about killing a lawman; for that matter any man. No, Brown's change of heart was down to his uncertainty about his ability to outdraw him.

Ike Brown spent most days in a ravine outside of town practising his draw. Latch-ford had happened upon him, and it had come as a shock to the marshal that, even now, Brown was faster. An old injury to his gunhand received during his cowpunching days had begun to act up. Arthritis had taken hold. His joints were stiffening. He had not been called upon to draw of late, but he feared that when he was his secret would be out at best, and at worst he'd be dead. And if he was still standing, Ike Brown would not waste time in throwing down the gauntlet.

Latchford was living on his reputation. But for how much longer? Brown was a swift-eyed honcho. Had he seen Latchford's slight fumble when he drew his pistol in the saloon just now? And if he had, would he recognize it for what it was?

Latchford, isolated by arrow-straight application of the law, had no one to confide in except Kate Trent, and he did not want to worry her. Of course, Doc Hockley knew, but he could trust the sawbones not to blabber.

Ike Brown was not the only threat. A Crichton hand with whiskey courage could throw down a challenge to ingratiate himself with Jody Crichton by removing the man who had, by common perception, stolen Kate Trent from the rancher.

Kate had stated unequivocally that she would lie down in a nest of vipers in preference to sharing Jody Crichton's bed. But Jody, just like his old man before him, never took no for an answer. Jody's statement that if he could not have Kate Trent, no other man would, had been as starkly unequivocal as Kate's rejection of him.

In fact, so vehement was Jody Crichton's spite, that Kate had been reluctant to accept Bob Latchford's proposal for fear of bringing harm to him.

'If you'll have me, I'm willing to take the chance, Kate,' Latchford had assured her. 'I reckon the prize far outweighs the risk.'

Bob Latchford, too, had pondered long and hard before asking Kate to marry him. Not out of fear of Jody Crichton – Kate had always been Cy Brodie's girl, and he had always been Cy's friend. It had taken time to shake his feeling of guilt in getting cosy with Kate. But with Cy gone and no sign of him coming back, he had finally summoned up the courage to pop the question.

Now, on the eve of his wedding, Cy Brodie was back. At least his ghost was. And that might prove every bit as powerful as his actual presence.


## CHAPTER NINE

After leaving Emily Wayne's shop, her emotions in turmoil, Kate Trent made her way to Sullivans Creek, the small creek outside of town where she had first set eyes on Cy Brodie trying to rope a stubborn steer. Kate recalled how flattered she had been when her sudden appearance had broken Cy's concentration. The steer, seizing its opportunity to set matters right with its tormentor, rammed Cy's horse and dislodged him from the saddle into the creek. Ever since that day she had always come to the creek to sit and ponder during troubled times, like the black day when Cy Brodie had been convicted of rustling.

On this occasion, Kate had come to try and sort out her doubts about marrying Bob Latchford, of whom she thought the world, but knew that that was far from the kind of loving commitment it would take to hold a marriage together. She did not want to be unfair to Bob, or indeed to herself either. Locked in a loveless marriage would be a cross that would likely break them both. Some marriages held together on friendship and respect, but worthy and as necessary as those were, Bob Latchford was a virile man who would want much more. Lying with Bob while thinking of Cy would be a torture to herself, and a cruelty to Bob Latchford which he did not deserve.

But was she in love with Cy Brodie? Or was she in love with the idea of being in love with him. She had fallen in love with Cy on their first meeting. But that was a long time ago. Until word had reached Bowen Crossing that the bank at neighbouring Gila Junction had been robbed by the Brodie gang, she had almost forgotten him, and had been quite happy to be Mrs Bob Latchford.

'Oh, maybe it's just your woman's heart, Kate,' she told her reflection in the sparkling water of the creek. 'Maybe you should have sense and put all thought of Cy Brodie right out of your silly head. He had his chance to ask you to marry him before he got in that bind with Ned Crichton, and he didn't.' Maybe, Kate thought, she had read more into Cy Brodie's attention to her than he had intended?

'Having second thoughts about shacking up with Latchford, Kate?'

Kate swung around on the boulder she was sitting on to look into Jody Crichton's sneering face. 'As if it's any of your darn business, Jody Crichton,' she spat.

'Everything you do will always be my business, Kate,' the rancher said. 'It's been that way since your first visit to the ranch.'

Kate Trent sprang up off the boulder. 'Aren't you ever going to get it through that head of yours that you and I are never–'

'Never is a long time, Kate,' Crichton interjected.

Kate strode to her horse, grumbling, 'Isn't there anywhere around here where a girl can get some peace and quiet?'

'The Crichton ranch,' he answered. 'Any time you want, Kate.' Kate was mounted up when Jody shrewdly asked, 'You having second thoughts with Cy Brodie in the neighbourhood?'

'Cy Brodie means nothing to me!'

'Look me in the eye and tell me that, Kate,' Crichton challenged. For a moment she did, but could not hold the rancher's knowing gaze. 'Brodie always sparked you like no other man could.' Bitterly, he said, 'Why you'd want to waste your time on a no-hoper the likes of Cy Brodie is a mystery to me.'

Against her better judgement, Kate flung back, 'It's easy to understand, Jody. There's no other man around here of equal measure to Cy Brodie.'

Sneering, the rancher asked, 'Does Latchford know that, Kate?' His sneer was replaced with a cunning smugness. 'Maybe now that I know, I might feel obliged to tell him how you feel.'

'You do that, Jody,' Kate Trent promised, 'and I'll kill you myself.'

Crichton's taunting laughter chased Kate out of the creek.

'Maybe you and Brodie could break rocks together,' he hollered after her.

On the ride back to town, Jody Crichton's parting words haunted her. Grudgingly, she conceded that he was right. What future was there to be had with a man on the owlhoot trail? Hiding out in roosts; always watching and waiting for a lawman or a posse to show, or a fast gun in some dingy town to explode. Other women had gone down that road, but had she the grit to follow? Did she really want to spend the rest of her days dodging?

By the time Kate reached town she had made up her mind. Spotting Marshal Latchford leaving his office looking none too pleased, Kate dismounted, walked right up to him, threw her arms around his neck, and kissed him like he'd never been kissed before.

Watching from the window of her dress-maker's shop, a dagger sank deep into Emily Wayne's heart. For a brief spell she had hoped that Kate would reject Bob Latchford, and had dreamed that the marshal might look her way. He did not know that Emily loved him; neither did Kate Trent. If it was one thing Emily could do better than dressmaking, it was keeping a secret.

Gabby Scanell came out of a hellish

nightmare in which he had dreamed that a vulture had plucked out his eyes and left him helpless. Sweat as thick as treacle covered every inch of his body. His hair, thickish for an oldster, clung wetly to his scalp. The fire in his gut was worse and clawed at his heart, making its beat uncertain.

It was deepest night. A quarter moon made the canyon an eerie, alien landscape. Had he heard something? Gabby was not sure. But his instincts, honed over his years of outlawry were seldom misguided. Were those shadows at the entrance to the canyon? Or were his fevered eyes playing tricks on him? He picked up the rifle which had slipped from his grasp, readying to give as good an account of himself as he could.

As the images firmed up and he was sure that he indeed had company, Gabby Scanell drew a shaky bead on the lead rider. The rifle's trigger was ninety per cent depressed when...

'Gabby?'

'Cy?' There was no denying the joy in the oldster's voice. Then, doubting his good fortune, Gabby quizzed, 'That really you, Cy?'

'It's me, Gabby.'

Brodie struck a lucifer. Its flickering light

added a new ghostliness to the rocky environs. The old man's delight doubled on seeing Bull Rankin.

'What're you fellas doin' here?' he asked. And, testily, 'Quench that damn match, Cy, before half the territory is headed our way.'

'Can see that your humour is still as prickly as when we left, Gabby,' Bull Rankin ribbed sociably.

On seeing the bundles of willow saplings, Gabby enquired, 'You fellas sellin' kindlin' now?'

Relieved on finding Gabby so feisty, Cy Brodie said, 'Good to see you're still alive and kicking, Gabby.'

Bull Rankin said good-humouredly, 'Reckon hell ain't ready yet for this cantankerous old bastard.'

'We've come to get you out of here,' Cy told the oldster.

Surprised, Gabby asked, 'Out?' He coughed and a trickle of blood showed on his lips. 'I ain't goin no place, Cy. 'Cept to my Maker.'

'Don't talk like that!' Brodie snapped. 'Do you want to die, old man?'

'No,' Scanell replied tetchily. 'But I ain't goin' to fool myself neither. I've got a bullet hole in me that's turned rotten, Cy. And I'm an old man whose energy is all spent. Put the two together and it ain't hard to figger out what my damn chances are.'

Regretting his outburst, Cy knelt alongside Gabby Scanell. His nostrils caught the stench of a wound gone bad, but he hid his revulsion.

'You listen to me, old man. Bull and me are going to make a sled with those willow saplings–'

'A sled?' Gabby yelped. 'You 'spect me to be hauled outa here like some darn cripple?'

'You're too weak to stay in a saddle,' Cy said. 'Want me and Bull to be bandaging your skull too, when you fall off your horse?'

'Never fell from a horse in my life,' the oldster said proudly. 'Not a horse 'round that could throw me!'

Cy Brodie grinned. 'Not if it knew that you'd get up and knock out every tooth it had.'

Scanell snorted. 'Would too, if the critter dumped me on my butt. And any horse I rode in my time knowed it. Like that mess of buzzard bait that brought me here knows I'll do when I find her.'

Cy did not tell Gabby Scanell that on the way into the canyon they had seen what was left of the mare after the vultures and mountain cats had finished with her.

'Heard some shootin' earlier,' Scanell said, 'a ways off.'

'A brush with a couple of Apaches,' Cy told the old man. 'Nothing to worry your head about, Gabby.'

''Paches. Nothin' to worry bout? 'Paches always need worryin' 'bout, Cy. 'Cause like rattlers, where there's one there's darn well sure to be more!'

Bull Rankin had started making the sled. A nimble-fingered weaver, he was making quick progress.

'Don't waste your time, Bull,' Scanell said. 'I ain't gettin' on no sled, and that's final.'

'Dammit, Gabby,' Cy Brodie exploded. 'Can't you get it through that skull of yours that getting to a doc is the only chance you've got?'

Gabby Scanell grimaced as another shaft of fire shot through his gut.

'What doc? Where?'

'Doc Hockley. In Bowen Crossing.'

'Bowen Crossin'?' Gabby exclaimed.

'Has that fever deadened your ears, too?' Cy growled.

Scanell who was privy to Cy Brodie's past, screwed up his sun-wrinkled face. 'That town is likely to string you up the second you show your face, Cy. You'd have to be loco to go anywhere near there. And don't depend on Bob Latchford to give you an easy ride: he's a lawman who goes by the book.'

'I won't be looking for any favours,' Cy said. 'I aim to have you down off this rock and in town before first light. I'm sorry, Gabby, but I'm going to have to drop you on Doc Hockley's doorstep and take off.'

'Anyone askin' me if'n I wanna go?' the old man argued. 'Well, I ain't!'

'You don't have a choice, Gabby,' Cy reasoned. 'That bullet has to come out of your gut, and fast.'

'Dyin' in jail ain't what I want, Cy.' Gabby's tired gaze went to the star-studded sky. 'If I can't get my darn harp from a four-poster bed, then I'll get it out here.'

Cy Brodie said resolutely, 'If that's the way you want it Gabby...'

'That's the way sure 'nuff,' Scanell confirmed.

'...then,' Cy said, 'I'll have to wait right here with you until you pass over.'

Gabby Scanell yelped, 'That's even more loco than ridin' into Bowen Crossin'!'

'You leave me no choice, Gabby. I won't ride on and leave you here alone, old man.'

'Well then.' Gabby Scanell put the rifle to

his head, 'I'll solve your problem for you right here and now.'

Quick as a rattler's spit, Cy kicked the gun out of the oldster's hand and told him, 'If you're not leaving here, I'm staying put, Gabby.'

The old man huffed and puffed, but there was no mistaking the light of pleasure in his eyes that someone should care enough to try and save his life. He conceded, 'I guess then, I'm goin' to have to climb 'board that damn sled!'

The sled completed, Brodie built a cocoon of rocks to shield the flame of a fire and brewed coffee. The desert night had a bite to it; the trek down the mountain would be energy sapping. He laced the scalding coffee with whiskey from a bottle he carried to ward off chills and disinfect any wounds that the gang might pick up.

'Get that inside you, Gabby,' he ordered the old-timer, handing him a tin cup of the fortified brew. 'Should keep out the cold for a spell.'

And ease the pain too, he hoped. He had given the old man more whiskey than coffee. When Gabby drank, a bout of coughing brought a trickle of blood to his lips, which he contemptuously wiped away with the cuff of his shirt sleeve.

On seeing the blood, Cy's worry hiked.

'What in tarnation did ya put in this coffee, Cy? Devil's piss?'

When Bull Rankin and Brodie had drunk their share of the strong brew, Cy cleansed and dressed Gabby Scanell's wound as best he could. He doused the fire and scattered its embers with his boot. Apaches could tell by the remains of a fire how long ago it had been lit, and from that an Indian could judge the approximate distance a man might have travelled.

Ready to set out on the crazy venture Cy Brodie had planned, Bull helped him put Gabby Scanell gently on to the sled. The old man had slipped back into unconsciousness, and his breathing was laborious. Hollows in his cheeks, which had not been there a short time before, were the kind a man gets when death beckons.

'He don't stand a chance of making it,' was Bull Rankin's opinion.

'That's not going to stop me trying, Bull,' was Cy Brodie's steely retort.

He secured the ropes of the sled to his saddlehorn, trailing them either side of the stallion. He would use the strength of his legs to keep the ropes as taut as he could to make Gabby's journey as trouble free as was possible. However, it would still be a jarring passage which would further weaken Gabby, if not finish him off altogether.

Worries piled up for Cy Brodie. If Gabby's condition worsened they might not be able to continue.

The old trail Cy had chosen as his route off the mountain might have fallen into disrepair and be too treacherous to negotiate, forcing him to ride the regular trail with all the risks that that would throw up.

Back at the creek, they had hidden the dead Apaches' bodies as best they could, but it would not take their comrades long to find them. Then they would come looking for their killer or killers.

Cy again told Rankin, 'This madness is of my choosing, Bull. An hour before sun-up you make tracks.'

'You bet, Cy.'

'Let's move out then.'

In the first couple of minutes of drawing the sled, Cy knew that he would be lucky if his tired horse stayed the course. As long as Bull Rankin was around they could switch the burden from mount to mount, but when Bull took off, the remaining miles to Bowen Crossing would be long and fraught.

If his horse went down, his and Gabby Scanell's bones would be bleached in the desert sun.

## CHAPTER TEN

Bob Latchford pondered his last night as a single man. He wondered if having a wife would change him? Change the way he got things done? Up to now, having responsibility only for himself, he had been able to take the risks necessary to enforce the law as it should be. But once wed, his actions would have to be tempered by the fact that he had a wife who depended on him. It troubled him that he might already be thinking differently. His mind went back to the saloon and Ethan Briscoe's trouble-stirring. He could remember a time when he would not have tolerated Briscoe's kind of rabble-rousing.

Hank Russell, the freight company owner, had offered him a job clerking.

'Think about it, Bob,' Russell had urged. 'A wife and a marshal's badge is an uneasy combination. And I need a good and trustworthy man to become part of a growing business.'

'I'm not a clerking kind of man, Hank,' Latchford had said.

'You'll get home safe nights. That'll make Kate easier in herself. It's a real burden on a woman being a lawman's mate, Bob. Fretting every time a gun goes off ages a woman fast.'

Maybe, Latchford thought, that he had been a tad too hasty in rejecting Hank Russell's offer.

Concern about being a married marshal was not the whole of Latchford's worry. He worried, too, about Kate Trent's hankering for Cy Brodie. Kate seemed to have overcome her pining, but he could not help wondering how she would react should Cy Brodie ride into town now, or one day in the future.

Gila Junction was only ten miles distant from Bowen Crossing. Ethan Briscoe had mentioned that one of the Brodie gang had caught lead in the bank raid. If Cy Brodie was the same caring man he had punched cows with, he would likely make tracks for Bowen Crossing with the wounded man, irrespective of the cost to himself. If it panned out that way, it would hand him one hell of a problem.

There was another factor – Jody Crichton. He was a man who did not take kindly to

84

rejection. And the fact that Kate had accepted Latchford's proposal of marriage, made him Crichton's automatic enemy. Only that very afternoon he had seen Jody Crichton in a huddle with Ike Brown near the livery. To the casual observer, it had looked like they were discussing the merits of a mare but to a man looking for signs of trouble, as Latchford was, their conversation about the mare was the pretext for a meeting for an entirely different purpose. But what purpose? Ike Brown's Judas glance at him had unnerved the marshal in a way that it would not have previously. But with a stiff gunhand and a new wife, any trouble was too much trouble.

Brown was a hothead, easily bought. He had a fondness for a full pocket, and no qualms about who filled it and why.

'Our marriage will be a cup of gall for Jody Crichton to drink, Bob,' Kate had warned. 'His pride will hurt. That will make him dangerous.'

'Nothing I can't handle,' Latchford had told her.

Recalling that statement now, Bob Latchford automatically flexed his fingers and grimaced at the shooting pain in his gunhand.

'Maybe you'll have damn all option but to accept that clerking job after all,' he growled.

Shaken out of his fevered sleep, Gabby Scanell gritted his teeth in an all out effort to keep from howling. Every bump, and there wasn't a foot of ground without one, sent shafts of searing pain through his gut no matter how hard Cy Brodie laboured to steady the sled. Their progress was ponderous, while the hours of the night flashed past in a wink.

Brodie brought the journey to a stop to give Gabby some relief. The red staining on Gabby's shirt was getting wider all the time.

'Leave me, Cy,' the old man pleaded. 'It'll be easier on me, and you won't be wastin' your time.'

His gaze settled on Bull Rankin. 'You tell him, Bull.'

Rankin did not speak, but an endorsment of Scanell's view was plainly there in his stance. Cy, too, despite his best efforts to remain hopeful, was beginning to believe that the task he had set himself was beyond him. The old trail was in no fit state. A couple of times they had been lucky not to have lost the sled over the edge when the trail suddenly crumbled. They were now on a straight, unprotected stretch of the trail with little or no cover. A strong wind had come up. It would rain soon, and when it did the water would rush down from higher up. If the rain was heavy enough it could wash them right off the trail.

He just had to make it to the flatter, tree-protected part of the steep trail before it rained. In his time he had seen trails vanish in a rain storm. If that happened at any part of the trail ahead he would be forced back up the trail. Or he might find himself caught between two breaks in the trail, one in front and one behind, hopelessly stranded and facing certain death.

Cy could also see that Bull Rankin was getting more uneasy by the second as the trail proved more difficult than his most pessimistic forecast. Brodie could not blame him if he cut his losses and took off. The odds were stacking against them.

'I'll hang tough for a spell longer,' was Rankin's reply, when Cy gave him the nod to make tracks for the border. 'But not for much longer, Cy,' he added sombrely. 'And if you have any sense, when I light out you'll do the same.'

Cy Brodie's response was dogged. 'While Gabby's got breath, I'll keep trying to get him to Doc Hockley's door, Bull.'

# CHAPTER ELEVEN

Jody Crichton left the ranch house with the sly stealth of a fox leaving a hen house. He made his way cautiously to the stables, pausing now and then to check the shadows around him. The moonlight was fitful, rainclouds racing across it driven by a strengthening wind. The ever changing pools of moonlight made the ranch yard an eerie landscape. It was the small hours of the morning, and it was unlikely that he would cross paths with anyone. But Jody would prefer not to have to explain his nocturnal ramblings. He became particularly cautious as he drew near to the bunkhouse. It was in total darkness, as it should be. But, being a Sunday morning, the Saturday night visit of the crew to town might put strain on bladders which would necessitate a trip to the privy. His caution proved correct as, suddenly, the bunkhouse door opened and a leathery old-timer who acted as cook and oddjob man came out quickly, holding his midriff. The rotgut served up on a Saturday night was of the lowest quality, and could be mighty hard on a man's innards. Jody took a step back into the shadows and bided his time until Joseph Murphy returned to the bunkhouse, still holding his gut and swearing that the following Saturday night he was not going anywhere near town.

Fat chance, Jody thought.

He waited a couple of minutes after the bunkhouse door slammed shut. Murphy's trip to the privy might have unsettled others who would follow him. After a time when no one showed, Jody continued on to the stables and saddled his horse. Then he tied some baling around the horse's hoofs to deaden their clop. Task finished, he edged out of the stables and rode out of the ranch yard watchfully. A safe distance on, he undid the baling and put it in his saddlebags to be used again on the return journey. Then he hit the trail for a line shack in the hills where he had arranged to meet up with Ike Brown to hand over the package stuffed inside his shirt.

'Won't last much longer, I reckon,' was Bull Rankin's opinion of Gabby Scanell's deteriorating condition. 'His breathing's getting more shallow with every second. Colour's bad too, Cy.'

In his frustration, Cy Brodie felt like telling Bull Rankin that he had eyes to see with but held his tongue. Rankin had shown fine qualities in turning back to help, and would be undeserving of the sharp end of his tongue.

'We're not going to make it to Bowen Crossing under cover of darkness, Bull,' Brodie said.

'No we ain't,' he agreed.

The rain had been brief and thankfully light. The wind had died and the cloud was slow moving, robbing them of the moon to light their way. Solid looking terrain could be illusory, and they might be stepping into a hole that would drop them to the craggy rocks at the base of the trail. Bull Rankin looked with concern to the night sky, still pitch black, but with threads of grey beginning to show in it.

'You'd best make tracks, Bull,' Cy advised. 'The border is only a couple of miles from here. You should be close to it by sun-up.'

Bull Rankin surprised himself with his response. 'There's time yet, Cy. Let's keep moving.'

Rankin reckoned that he might have already left it a mite late to run for the border. He worried about the stretch of open country which he would have to cross to enter Mexico at the remote point he had chosen. With the American and Mex authorities wrangling over the two-way traffic of outlaws, both governments had despatched their soldiers to patrol the border. It was an impossible task. The border was long and ragged, with a man often not knowing which side of it he was on until Mex or American soldiers or lawmen put in an appearance. By then it was often too late. Indians, too, dogged the border, raiding up out of Mexico and then fleeing back with the cavalry on their tails.

American lawmen or soldiers would incarcerate him. Mex soldiers would likely string him up, while the Apaches, if time allowed, would kill him slowly.

Glumly, Bull Rankin thought, some choice, some options.

Cy Brodie slapped Rankin on the shoulder. 'You're as loco as they come, Bull. But I surely thank you for your help.'

Kate Trent sat at her bedroom window looking at the fickle moon pondering on the next night when, for the first time, she would share her bed with Bob Latchford, indeed with any man. She wondered if Bob would be a caring and considerate lover? Her courtship had held no fears for her. Bob had always been a perfect gentleman, though to her shame there was a time or two when she had wished otherwise.

Kate had gone to bed as contented as a queen bee in her hive, her mind firmly settled on becoming Mrs Bob Latchford. But she dreamed of Cy Brodie. Now she was sitting, looking into the night, unable to put Cy from her mind. Her actions were not, Kate was acutely aware, those of a woman taking vows the next day. Deeply unhappy, Kate murmured, 'Oh, Cy. Why have you never shown up and settled my mind on whether you love me or not?'

On hearing the sound of hoofs, Ike Brown hurried to the door of the line shack to see Jody Crichton ride up.

'You took your sweet time, Crichton,' the budding gunfighter moaned. 'It's as cold as a Yukon winter in this damn shack.'

Jody, not used to the kind of disrespect Brown showed him, strained at the leash to curb his temper. Most men kow-towed to the powerful rancher, but Ike Brown was different. He owed the rancher nothing, or had everything to gain from licking his boots. Crichton thought himself way superior to Brown and would normally not have spat in his direction, let alone consort with him. But if he wanted the job he had in mind done without dirtying his own hands, he needed Ike Brown.

'Kind of jumpy, ain't you,' Crichton taunted. 'If you're not up to–'

'I'm up to doin' what you want done, Crichton, so long as you're willin' to pay for the doin' of it.'

The rancher reached inside his shirt and withdrew the bulky package he had stashed there. He undid the brown-paper wrapping of the package and threw the contents on to the table. Dollar bills spilled across the table.

'A thousand dollars; as agreed.'

On seeing the spill of bills, Ike Brown's eyes widened. His grasp was greedy. He examined the bills closely, as if suspecting chicanery on Crichton's part. He had never seen a thousand dollars in one batch before, and had never expected that the rancher would meet his demand without quibble.

His greedy eyes met Jody Crichton's. The rancher's handing over of a thousand dollars so readily, showed how anxious he was to stop Latchford marrying Kate Trent. Brown saw an opportunity to add to his pot.

'I've been thinking, Crichton...'

The rancher snorted. 'I bet you have.'

'I reckon that riskin' my neck goin' up against Latchford is worth another...' – he feigned thought about a figure he had already settled on – 'thousand.'

Jody Crichton was tempted to go for his gun and teach Brown a lesson he'd never forget. A couple of bullets in his kneecaps might remind him of his stupidity for the rest of his miserable life. However, he was in a bind, and Brown knew it. He could not soil his hands in challenging Latchford himself. If he did so, Kate Trent would turn her face against him forever – if he was still around for her to despise him. So, if he wanted the marshal dispatched, while retaining a chance of earning Kate's favour down the line, his hand could not be seen in Latchford's killing.

Everyone knew that Brown was working up the grit to face the marshal. So when he did, folk would see his challenge as the end result of a long held ambition, and that suited Crichton perfectly.

He had no alternative but to agree to Ike Brown's terms, but not so readily as to alert Brown to the fact that he was prepared to pay any sum he might be of a mind to demand to stop Bob Latchford marrying Kate Trent.

Crichton scoffed. 'Another thousand, huh?'

'I figure,' Brown replied.

The rancher took comfort from the quiver in the no-good's voice. Crichton, an expert haggler like his father before him, now knew that he could faze Brown.

'Forget it!'

He gathered up the bills on the table.

Ike Brown felt a rising panic as he watched Crichton wrap the bills and stuff them back inside his shirt. His panic dried him up inside. Never again would he have his hands on a thousand dollars. It was his ticket out of town to places he had dreamt about; places like Dodge City and Tombstone, where he could make the reputation he craved. But how far could he push Crichton? He knew that the rancher could not soil his hands with Bob Latchford's blood. If he did Kate Trent would shun him like the plague.

'Fifteen hundred,' he chanced.

Jody Crichton shook his head.

'Seems fair to me,' Brown argued, but not confidently.

Crichton made a show of considering Brown's argument, but he had already made up his mind that Ike Brown would settle for little more than what was already on offer.

'Twelve hundred, tops,' the rancher haggled.

Rather than squeeze Crichton and risk losing out completely, Ike Brown settled. 'Twelve hundred,' he agreed.

Crichton put five hundred back on the table. 'The rest comes when the job's done.'

'That ain't fair,' Brown yelped.

'Take it or leave it,' Crichton drawled, clawed hand ready to sweep up the bills once more.

Brown tussled with himself.

'Make up your mind, Brown. Deal or not?'

Sullenly, Ike Brown mumbled, 'Deal.'

Jody Crichton's smile was cocky. 'Nice doing business with you, Ike.'

The rancher left the line shack pleased with his night's work, relishing the secret pleasure of putting a bullet in Ike Brown's back as soon as he killed Latchford. Before they parted company, Jody Crichton checked, 'Are you sure you're fast enough to take Latchford?'

Ike Brown's mood was expansive. 'I'm sure.'

Brown's thoughts went back a couple of days. Taking a short cut home through the town's backlots, he had passed by Doc

Hockley's office. The doc's office window was open. Latchford was his patient. Brown crept up to the open window to eavesdrop on a mighty interesting conversation between Hockley and Latchford.

'The arthritis in your right hand from that old injury is getting worse all the time, Bob. I'm not sure how long more you'll be able to handle a gun the way a lawman needs to. If that cur Ike Brown were to square up to you now...'

Brown's smile was snake-oil smooth.

'Latchford's a dead man!' he assured Crichton confidently.


## CHAPTER TWELVE

Cy Brodie's luck improved. The brief rainfall made Gabby Scanell's sled easier to haul. The steeper part of the trail was behind them, and he made swift progress down the lower part. The flat desert terrain was reached sooner than seemed probable an hour previously. But the galling fact of the matter was that Gabby Scanell had weakened considerably. It was a miracle that

he had lasted this long, but even if Cy succeeded in getting him to Bowen Crossing
still sucking air, it was unlikely that he
would survive now.

Cy Brodie made a decision which would
cost him his freedom, maybe even his life.

'He's in mighty poor shape, Cy,' Bull
Rankin murmured, neither man sure if the
unconscious Scanell could hear them. 'I
reckon you're flogging a dead horse.'

For the first time, Cy Brodie agreed.

'I guess getting Gabby to Bowen Crossing
on time was a pipe dream from the start,
Bull.'

'You did your best,' Rankin said. 'But now
it's time to make Gabby as comfortable as
we can and head for the border.'

'Bull is making a whole lot of sense, Cy.'
Surprised, Brodie and Rankin spun around.
The old-timer was smiling at them weakly,
his smile bereft of its normal impishness.
His grey eyes had sunk further into their
sockets, and their fire was fading. 'Just leave
me a gun, fellas.'

Deep in depression because of his failure
to save his friend, for the briefest of
moments Cy almost agreed to Gabby
Scanell's request, until the grit which had
seen him through many a crisis since Ned

Crichton's treachery had corkscrewed his life came to the fore.

'We're headed for Bowen Crossing, old man,' he told Gabby. 'And that's an end of this wrangling of yours! You hear me?'

Bull Rankin had made up his mind. 'This is as far as I go, Cy.'

'I understand, Bull. I thank you for your help.' He looked to the paling sky. 'I sure hope you make it to that Mex roost.'

Rankin said, 'I'll make it.' He swung his horse and pointed the mare towards the border. 'See you fellas soon.'

He spurred the horse to a quickish pace; a pace which was too fast for the difficult terrain, but time was running against him, and risks had to be taken. Though he had cockily declared that he would make it to Mexico, his gut feeling told him otherwise. He was not worried about the Gila Junction posse – if they were still giving chase – his concern was for the dreaded Apache. With the posse it was likely that his death would be quick, a rope slung over the nearest tree. But with the Indians...

Rankin shuddered.

Cy Brodie mounted his own horse and set his sights firmly on Bowen Crossing. Drawing the sled would be more difficult and precarious without Bull Rankin's help, but he had the advantage of knowing the country he was travelling through.

In hostile terrain that was a distinct plus.

Ethan Briscoe was up early. The lumpy bed he had had to lie on was a far cry from the feather bed in which he spent his nights in Gila Junction, a town whose dust he had been planning on shaking off with the town funds in his pocket until, out of the blue, good fortune had smiled on him. A drunk passing through town, who had been a Confederate captain in the war, told him about the very special cargo be had been put in charge of escorting in the last weeks of the war.

A press and plates to forge Union dollar bills.

'The plan was to forge Union bills to undermine the North's economy,' the drunk had confided to Briscoe. 'A really smart scheme. Would probably have worked too, if the South hadn't run out of time.'

Ethan Briscoe was about to call the proprietor of the café in which he was lunching to have the drunk removed from his table, where he had sat down uninvited a couple of minutes earlier. Now he changed his mind.

'Kind of interesting story for a banker, isn't it?' the drunk had slurred. 'Alarming, too. All those fake dollars floating around the place.'

'Interesting,' was Briscoe's casually lazy response, as if indulging the drunk. It wouldn't do to show the kind of interest that was tightening his gut.

It was a cat and mouse game.

'The press and those plates never made it through,' the drunk said.

Briscoe waited, making a show of eating his food, though it was piling up against a knotted gut.

'Me and Fred Defoe were the only survivors of an Indian attack...'

The banker sipped his wine.

'Defoe caught lead down Nogales way last year. Which...' – Briscoe fought to keep his breathing even – 'leaves only me knowing where that press is, Mr Briscoe.'

'Mighty interesting tale, Mr...?'

'Rose. Daniel Rose at your service, sir.'

'...But I'm a busy man,' Briscoe said. 'So, if you'll excuse me, I'll finish my lunch and be on my way.'

Taken aback, Rose asked, 'You're not interested?'

'Like I said, an interesting tale, but–'

'You've got your lunch to finish,' Rose said, his mood testy.

'That's right, Mr Rose.'

Daniel Rose licked parched lips. Ethan Briscoe took his cue. His rummaged in his pocket, but came up clean-fingered.

'I don't carry cash; I have an account here at the café. But–' the banker's eyes held Rose's – 'if you'd be of a mind to drop by the bank in a while I'll be glad to reward you for entertaining me during my lunch.'

The tale-teller's eyes lost their deadness and sparkled. 'Yeah? What kind of reward would that be, Mr Briscoe?'

Ethan Briscoe smiled his most beatific smile, which had many times got him out of corners he had no right to escape from. He said, 'I'm not an ungenerous man, Mr Rose.'

The drunk grinned. 'That a fact, Mr Briscoe.'

'Later, then?'

'Yeah. Later,' Rose agreed.

Ethan Briscoe's life had had many turning points, but none as fortuitous as the one handed to him by the drunk now shuffling out of the café, leaving the banker's mind spinning in all sorts of heady directions. He waited a couple of minutes before leaving,

102

but could not eat another bite.

'Grub not to your liking, Ethan?' the café proprietor asked, on seeing a plate which had not as usual been picked clean.

'It was a fine lunch, Mollie,' the bank president told the café owner. He massaged his considerable gut. 'It's just that I've picked up a queasy tummy. See you same time tomorrow.'

'I won't put this on your tab,' Mollie called after him.

'Appreciate that, Mollie,' he called back.

When he stepped out of the café door, Briscoe forced himself to walk in his usual ambling stroll back to the bank. Daniel Rose would probably be watching, to monitor any excitement on his part, so it was vitally necessary to show none. The banker did not wish to convey to Rose the heart-stopping importance of his revelations. He stopped to chat, and shared a joke with Sam Benton, the livery owner. When he reached the bank, he paused outside to light a cigar and puffed on it in a leisurely fashion before entering.

Inside, he kept up his carefully contrived pose, passing the time of day and greetings to the few customers transacting business; the nickel-and-dime kind of business that the Gila Junction bank did, and which Ethan Briscoe had grown tired of. But Daniel Rose's tale had now changed all that. New money-spinning plans were filling Briscoe's head.

Once inside his office, Ethan Briscoe gave his exuberance free rein. He gasped for breath, and hurried to get the bottle of French brandy in his desk drawer. He poured a generous drink and slugged the brandy down in one go. When it hit the spot, he trembled from head to toe with the release of the tension which had gripped him. He slumped into the plush chair behind his desk, poured another drink, and slugged it back in one gulp. Slowly, his twanging nerves settled.

He lay back in his chair, eyes closed, breathing deeply. His composure was just about restored when his teller poked his head round the office door.

'What is it, Chambers?' Briscoe enquired casually, as he had done a thousand times before in the three years he'd been president of the bank.

'Fella insisting on seeing you, Mr Briscoe...'

'What's so unusual in that?'

'Not our usual kind of caller,' Chambers said. 'He's a drunk.'

'Lower your voice,' Briscoe rebuked his teller. 'A customer is a customer, Chambers. Show the gentleman in.'

'Huh?'

'I said–'

'I know what you said, Mr Briscoe, but maybe if you come and looksee first?'

'Show him in,' Briscoe snapped.

'Sure, Mr Briscoe. I'll be right outside the door if you need any help.'

'You,' the banker ordered, 'will attend to your duties. I am well able to take care of myself, Chambers.'

'It's your funeral,' the teller muttered, as he turned away. He called out to Daniel Rose, 'Mr Briscoe will see you now.'

A moment later, the drunk stepped past Chambers into Briscoe's office, jittery with the need for a bottle.

'Your duties, Chambers,' the banker reminded the teller when he was inclined to linger.

The office door closed.

'Sit,' Briscoe invited Daniel Rose.

The former Confederate captain's eyes greedily settled on the bottle of French brandy on Briscoe's desk. The banker poured, filling the glass to the rim. He pushed the glass across the desk tantalizingly slow, holding back on the last couple of inches.

'Let's talk first, Mr Rose,' he said.

## CHAPTER THIRTEEN

Shortly after Bull Rankin lit out in the grey morning light, Cy Brodie spotted an Apache hunting party. They were some way off, but he could not risk their paths crossing. The sun would soon burst on the horizon. Not long after that the rain in the sandy soil would evaporate, and his horse's hoofs and the sled would send up a cloud of dust which would be readily seen by the Indians.

He would bet that by now they had found their slain colleagues at the creek. Their blood would be up. The cavalry had them on the run, too. They would wreak as much carnage as they could as they fled back to Mexico.

Brodie had by now given up all hope of Gabby Scanell surviving. But if the old man made it breathing to Bowen Crossing, Cy was determined to see his new scheme for Gabby through. On arrival in town, he would book Gabby into the Silver Chandelier hotel, and let him die in the four-poster he had always dreamed of. If Gabby expired before that, Cy was equally determined to see his old friend get the kind of funeral which he could boast about in the hereafter. And any man, including Bob Latchford, who stood in his way would have to kill him to prevent him seeing his plan through.

The man in Cy Brodie's thoughts had at that moment made a decision he had been avoiding for a long time. He was on his way to Hal Mannion's house, (his sometime deputy when, on the odd occasion, his duties took him out of town for a day or so) to tell Mannion that he planned on handing over the marshal's badge to him after his wedding, having decided to take up Hank Russell's offer of clerking.

'Howdy, Bob,' Mary Mannion greeted the marshal.

'Hal home, Mary?'

'Sure. Not expecting trouble, are you, Bob?' she fretted.

Thankfully, Hal Mannion's appearance from the hen house saved him having to answer.

'Why concern yourself, Bob,' Kate Trent

had asked the night before when, under her questioning, Latchford had confided his fears to her about the trouble he reckoned was headed their way, 'you'll be on your honeymoon.'

Though Kate's tone had been light and airy, her thoughts were dark, her heart constricted by fear; fear that Cy Brodie and Bob Latchford, her husband to be, and the man whom she could not, despite her staunchest efforts, dislodge from her mind, would come face to face.

One man would apply the law fearlessly and without favour; the other would be left with the choice of going to prison for long years, or taking on the man whose plan it was to imprison him.

Bob Latchford's worries were plenty. Added to the pile was what Kate's reaction would be if Cy Brodie showed up. Cy still occupied a special place in Kate Trent's heart. What he was unsure of was the divide: how much did he occupy? How much did Cy Brodie own?

'Fresh pot of coffee on the stove, Bob?' Mary Mannion invited.

It remained a complete mystery to most folk in Bowen Crossing, as to how a man with a beanpole frame and a dial that would scare a ghost, had put his brand on a woman as beautiful as Mary Mannion. Latchford had concluded a long time ago, that it had to be Hal Mannion's inner rather than outer qualities which had attracted Mary. Those fine inner qualities of honesty and gentleness were as glowing in Hal Mannion, as his exterior qualities were unprepossessing.

'Obliged, Mary,' Latchford said, following her through to the bright and airy kitchen, in a house that was always cleaner than a new pin.

Mary poured the coffee, and offered the marshal a plate of freshly baked biscuits. She went to the window and opened it, letting in the rain fresh breeze.

'Not often we get the chance to breathe anything but dust, Bob.'

Mary Mannion was, as usual, her sociable self. But her hazel eyes were clouded by worry. Talk around town about the Brodie gang being close by and likely to head their way had given her a sleepless night. Bob Latchford turning up on her doorstep for Hal had notched up her anxiety even further.

Mary asked mischievously, 'Looking forward to being a lassoed man, Bob?'

Latchford laughed. 'You only have to lasso an unwilling steer, Mary. I'm more than willing to walk right into Kate's corral.'

Mary Mannion sat to the table. 'Heard Cy Brodie's on our doorstep?'

'Seems so.'

The marshal made his answer casually conversational, hiding any hint of his concern.

'Robbed the bank at Gila Junction, they say?'

'Looks that way, Mary.'

'They say Brodie might come here to Bowen Crossing, Bob?'

Latchford shrugged, and willed Hal Mannion, who had gone to tidy up, to put in an appearance. Mary Mannion was a shrewd and keenly intelligent woman who was more than capable of unearthing his worries.

'Probably won't matter anyway,' Mary speculated. 'I hear the banker whose bank the Brodie gang robbed is rounding up men to hunt them down.'

'That's the plan,' Latchford confirmed.

Mary Mannion's hazel eyes trapped Latchford's blue.

'Bob, I worry about Hal wearing a badge, even on the odd occasion you call upon him.' Her eyes clouded with worry. 'Hal is not ... well, you know what I mean, I'm sure?'

He did. And Latchford knew that Mary's

fears were well founded. Hal Mannion had a lot of fine skills, but using a gun effectively was not one of them.

Mary Mannion's fingers fretted her reddish hair. 'Thank heavens you'll only be gone a week.'

'Well, Mary–'

'Howdy, Bob.' Hal Mannion came into the kitchen rubbing his hands on a towel. 'Expecting trouble, I hear?'

Bob Latchford shrugged. 'Nothing I can't handle, Hal.'

Latchford had changed his mind about handing over his badge to Hal Mannion, not having the heart to add to Mary Mannion's worry.

'Then why...?'

The marshal chuckled. 'Heck, Bob. I was passing and got the whiff of fresh biscuits.'

'A sensible fella, the marshal,' Mary Mannion said, her relief palpable.

'Then you don't need me?' Hal asked.

'Maybe if Cy Brodie and his partners show up, Hal.'

Mannion's disappointment eased. 'I sure need the pay, Bob. Looks like those darn chickens have gone on strike.'

Mary Mannion hugged her husband. 'We'll get by like we always do, Hal.'

'My guess is that the Brodie gang is long since across the border,' Latchford opined. 'Can't see any good reason why they would want to hang around with Apaches on the prowl.'

'I don't know much about Cy Brodie, Bob. He had just gone on the run from the law when Hal and I moved here. But from what I understand he's not the kind of man to leave a partner to die.'

Mary Mannion was well informed.

'No, Mary,' the marshal agreed, 'he's not.'

'If that's the case,' Mary reasoned, 'if his partner is still alive...'

Latchford saw no point in trying to pull the wool over Mary Mannion's eyes. She was much too intelligent a woman for that.

'Yes,' the marshal admitted, 'it's likely that if that's the case, Cy Brodie will try and get help for his friend. And around here we've got the only and the finest sawbones in Ben Hockley. Cy will know that.'

'You and Brodie were friends, weren't you, Bob?' Hal Mannion asked.

'The best,' Latchford said.

'What made Brodie go bad?' The question was Mary Mannion's.

'He was found guilty of rustling,' the marshal said.

'Sounds to me,' Mary speculated, 'that you don't rightly believe that, Bob.'

The Bowen Crossing lawman shrugged. 'Just let's say that back then, Cy Brodie would be the last man in these parts that I'd have branded as dishonest.'

Hal Mannion said, 'Leaves you with something of a dilemma if Brodie shows up here, don't it?'

Grimly, Bob Latchford answered, 'No dilemma, Hal. If Cy Brodie puts in an appearance in Bowen Crossing, I'll sling him back in jail. That's what the law requires me to do, and that's what I'll darn well do!'

The marshal stood up.

'Thanks for the coffee and biscuits, Mary.'

'My pleasure. I'll see you out.'

'You holler if you need me, Bob,' Hal Mannion called after them.

In the hall, Mary Mannion said, 'Thanks for leaving Hal out of this, Bob.' Then: 'Folk say that the Gila Junction bank wasn't worth raiding. That right?'

'More leaves on a late fall tree than dollars in the Gila Junction bank, I reckon,' the marshal affirmed.

'Then why would the Brodie gang raid it?' Mary speculated. 'And why is that Gila Junction banker risking his hide in hostile

113

country to retrieve so little?'

Bob Latchford grinned. 'Two good questions, Mary. Wish I had the darn answers to them.'

'A real puzzler, huh?'

'That,' Bob Latchford replied, 'it surely is, Mary.'

Latchford left the Mannion house an uneasy man, his troubles mounting by the second. As he strolled to the freight depot to tell Hank Russell of his temporary change of plans, (because it was still his intention to hand in his badge once the present climate of danger passed) his mind was given over to thinking about postponing his wedding until calmer times, because, should events pan out in an ugly fashion, Kate could end up a widow on the very day she became a bride.

His preoccupation with his thoughts brought Latchford almost face to face with Ike Brown before he became aware of his presence. The budding gunfighter blocked his path in a menacing stance that rang alarm bells in the marshal.

'Something troubling you, Ike?'

Bob Latchford's casual tone of enquiry belied the fear stalking him. It looked like Ike Brown had at long last got up the grit to throw down the gauntlet.

Latchford flexed the fingers of his gunhand. The action sent arrows of pain shooting into his wrist.

He wasn't at all sure if he would be standing seconds from now.

## CHAPTER FOURTEEN

Cy Brodie took shelter in a gully as the Apache hunting party drew near. The furnace heat of the refuge would not allow him to remain there for long. The fetid stench from the carcass of a rotting mountain cat filled the narrow hiding place and snatched Brodie's breath away. Tiredness, deepening all the time, threatened to overwhelm him, and his head throbbed with pain fit to split open his skull.

Gabby Scanell was in a deep coma, and looked unlikely to revive again. But he had before, and as a sensible precaution Cy remained ready to clamp his hand over the old-timer's mouth should he come to. If he had to do such a thing, even for the briefest time, it would be the end of Gabby Scanell's life, but Cy figured that he had no choice. A rumpus in the desert stillness would have Indians crawling all over him.

Emily Wayne watched from the window of her dressmaker's shop as Bob Latchford strolled to the freight depot, her heart full of grief that before the day was out he would be Kate Trent's husband. She had a crazy notion to flee the store, confront the marshal, and spill her heart to him. The appearance of Ike Brown from an alley to block Bob Latchford's path put a brake on her impulse. Just as well, too, she thought. Bob would likely have thought her crazy. But wasn't she? Crazy with love for him.

Brown and the marshal were talking, but there was something in Ike Brown's gait that alerted Emily. Suddenly, alarmed by her conclusion, Emily grabbed the rifle from under the shop counter and raced out of the door. She knew for certain that Ike Brown was about to draw on Bob Latchford, and she also knew by some ancient instinct that Latchford was doomed.

'Duck, Bob!' Emily Wayne screamed.

Latchford spun around. 'Stay out of it, Emily!'

Brown's gun flashed from leather. It spat.

Latchford clutched at his left arm. Had he not turned towards the dressmaker, the bullet would have had far more serious consequences. A clear path opened up between Ike Brown and Emily Wayne. Ike Brown showed no mercy. His .45 bucked, and Emily was swept off her feet. Latchford's sixgun blasted Ike Brown in the opposite direction. As Brown tried to get up, the incensed lawman showed no mercy either. His sixgun bucked again. Ike Brown's guts spilled out through the gaping hole in his belly.

People were crowding around Emily Wayne. Doc Hockley was rushing to help the dressmaker, but Latchford knew that it was all in vain. Emily had been caught square in the chest. He knelt beside her and took her in his arms.

'Hell, Emily, why did you do such a fool thing?'

The remaining seconds of the dressmaker's life were happy ones. She had achieved at last what she had been seeking for so long: she was in Bob Latchford's arms. She took her happiness with her into eternity.

Latchford stood up, his face set in stone. It was as he had feared. Trouble with a capital

T had come to Bowen Crossing.

Relieved, Cy Brodie watched the Indians ride into the distance. Fortunately, Gabby had not revived during the Apaches' passage, but he stirred now. Cy doused his neckerchief with the little water left in his canteen. He wet the oldster's lips and face.

Scanell's rolling eyes opened, filled with confusion and tears.

'Mikey?' he croaked. Delighted, he grabbed Cy's hands. 'Never figgered I'd set eyes on you again.' Having learned Gabby's history over the trails, Brodie knew that the man he thought he was seeing was his brother Mikey, who had died of consumption when he was eighteen years old. Gabby had often pondered on what his life might have been like had his older brother lived.

'Me and Mikey had great plans,' Gabby had confided to Brodie. 'We was goin' to Canada to grow the finest damn wheat a man ever growed.'

'How's Ma, Mikey?' Gabby enquired urgently.

'Ma's just fine,' Cy reassured the old man.

'That darn hip still actin' up somethin' awful?'

'No,' Cy said. 'Not that you'd notice, Gabby.'

'Gabby?' Scanell asked in surprise. 'You used to never call me nothin' but Gabriel, Mikey.'

Cy gambled. 'You never did like being called *Gabriel*, that I recall?'

Gabby Scanell's eyelids fluttered. 'Never did at that,' he murmured, and slipped back into unconsciousness. Cy made him as comfortable as was possible on the roughly made sled, which had stood up surprisingly well to the rigours of the trail.

The outlaw froze on hearing the clatter of shale behind him. He spun around just in time to see a blur of movement. An Apache tail scout, whom he should have counted on, was coming at him, tomahawk poised to strike.

## CHAPTER FIFTEEN

Resisting the urge to use his six-gun as a quick fix solution, Cy dived to his right. A gunshot would have the Apache hunting party all over him in no time at all.

119

The slashing tomahawk met a rock inches from Cy Brodie's head. A shower of diamond bright sparks fanned out from the contact of steel against stone. The Apache's lunge carried him to a lower level in the gully, head first. But the hope that Cy had of the Indian opening his skull on a rock was short lived when, with the agility of a mountain cat, the Apache twisted acrobatically in midair and landed on his feet. Cy knew that luck was not running his way when the Indian landed on sandy, stone-free soil, as soft as a feather pillow.

The tomahawk's shaft had split in two on impact with the rock and had been rendered useless. However, the hunting knife the Apache now pulled from his belt was every bit, if not more, deadly.

The Indian circled Cy, smug in the knowledge that Brodie's pistol had to remain silent if he wanted to avoid alerting the hunting party. Grinning evilly, the Apache put the blade of the hunting knife to his throat and drew an imaginary slit across from ear to ear, leaving Cy in no doubt as to his plans for his demise.

Cy Brodie growled, 'Come on then, you murdering bastard!'

Kate Trent took the news of Emily Wayne's death badly. Emily and she had been friends from the first day Kate had arrived in Bowen Crossing. Emily's death put a black streak in a day which should have been Kate's happiest.

'Maybe we should call off the nuptials, Kate?' Latchford suggested.

'That's the last thing Emily would want,' Kate declared spiritedly. Latchford shuffled uneasily.

'You want to marry me, don't you?' Kate asked, stunned by the marshal's seeming reluctance to go ahead with the wedding. 'Bob...?'

'Sure I do, Kate,' he said. 'But...'

'But what?'

'Well, with this air of trouble brewing...'

Kate asked, 'Cy Brodie kind of trouble, Bob?'

Doc Hockley who had been privy to their conversation dismissed this idea out of hand. 'Brodie's never been back since he busted out of jail. Why would he pick now to...' The sawbones let his voice trail off.

'Go on, Doc,' Bob Latchford pressed. 'Say what you've got in mind.'

Kate Trent was suddenly uneasy with that request. Hockley, normally a man given to

121

stating his views plainly and bluntly, was having immense trouble with what he had to say now.

'Well...' he began, his eyes darting between Kate and Latchford. 'I mean... What I...'

His gaze had by now settled on Kate.

Kate said, 'Like Bob says, Doc. Out with it.'

'OK,' the medico said resolutely. 'It's your wedding day, Kate. Brodie could have heard about it on the trails. And that, for a man who loved you more than his own life, could be a mighty good reason for him to pay a visit.'

'Cy never declared his love for me, Doc,' Kate said.

'Didn't have to,' Hockley said brusquely. 'He wore his heart on his sleeve. And,' Hockley emphasized, 'if it's true that one of the gang caught lead in the bank raid, Cy Brodie will not be found wanting in trying to get help for the man.'

Kate's glance went to Bob Latchford. She felt his eyes search her soul.

'Maybe, Kate,' he said, 'you're marrying the wrong man.'

Bob Latchford turned and left the infirmary.

'Heck,' the medico groaned. 'Me and my

big mouth.'

Kate sagged in the chair she was sitting on. 'I guess the wedding is off, Doc.'

Treading on eggs, Cy Brodie circled the Apache, but the circle was closing all the time. Cy grabbed a rock and slung it at the Indian, but he ducked the missile with ease, his muscular, lithe body honed to perfection for taking evasive action in the face of a threat. His cruel eyes mocked Brodie. The Apache danced in and out of the circle, taunting him, in no hurry to finish Brodie off. The Apache was only too aware of Cy Brodie's predicament. He had a gun that was useless. He could, of course, as a last resort use it. But the Apache knew that he could not lose. If Cy used the gun, he would sign his death warrant anyway. And to the Apache, all that mattered was that the land of his ancestors would have one less white man to desecrate its sacredness.

Besides, if the white man went for his gun, he would sling the knife. His skill with a knife was second nature to him. He even had the spot where he would embed it picked out.

Right in what the white man called his Adam's apple.

# CHAPTER SIXTEEN

Ethan Briscoe stormed into the law office.

'Why the hell did you kill Ike Brown, Marshal?' he demanded.

In no humour to suffer the banker's tirade, Bob Latchford grabbed a fistful of his fancy shirt and slammed him up against the door he had just bulled his way through.

'Because he needed killing!' he growled.

Following, equally irate Briscoe's Gila Junction cohorts were stopped dead in their tracks by Latchford's show of anger. Latchford, a man of controlled emotions, was now ashamed of his outburst. He let his grip on the banker go, and went to sit in the chair behind his desk. His temper in hand, he observed, 'Don't understand why you fellas are so fired up about the Brodie gang—'

Ethan Briscoe, the immediate danger to his person in abeyance, interjected hotly, 'They robbed my bank. For me that's reason good enough, Marshal Latchford.' He waved his hand over his partners. 'And these fellow business associates suffered losses, too. Their money was in my bank.'

Latchford's gaze wandered from one man to the next.

'Still don't understand why you're so het up?' he said. 'I know Gila Junction.' His gaze settled on Ethan Briscoe. 'I know the bank, too. And I reckon that the entire takings of that town wouldn't be enough to pay for a good barn dance.'

'Nonsense, Marshal,' Briscoe protested.

'Maybe,' Latchford said. 'But in my book it's a reasonable enough assessment of the Gila Junction bank's worth.' Latchford frowned. 'What I don't understand is how Cy Brodie thought there was rich pickings in your bank to begin with?'

Try as they might, the group could not hide their collective unease at Latchford's keen interest in their affairs.

'It's a question I'll have to ask Cy if he comes this way, I guess,' the marshal said.

Briscoe exclaimed, 'Brodie's coming here?'

'I reckon he is,' Latchford said.

'How do you know that, Marshal?' one of Briscoe's partners, the Gila Junction general storekeeper asked.

'You got proof?' a second man, the Gila Junction saloon owner wanted to know.

Latchford rubbed his belly. 'In here, gents. That's my proof.'

Briscoe scoffed, 'That, Marshal Latchford, is no proof at all.'

Bob Latchford said, 'Me and Cy Brodie used to be peas in a pod, Briscoe. We could tell what was in each other's minds before we knew ourselves, that's how close we were in the old days before Cy got in a tangle with Ned Crichton.'

The lawman became reflective.

'The correctness of which I have long doubted. You see, I never really believed that Cy Brodie was a rustler. There was no reason why Cy should suddenly go bad. Another month or two, when he got the gumption to pop the question, Cy would have been marrying the woman I was suppose to marry today. So it made no sense at all that he should throw away such a prize as Kate Trent.'

Bob Latchford shook his head. 'Not for all the cattle in the territory!'

There was a long silence before the marshal asked Briscoe, 'Have you got a posse ready to ride?'

'That I do,' the banker confirmed. Then Briscoe's face took on a look of cunning, which was never far below the surface. 'But

126

with Brodie headed this way, maybe' – his eyes took in his partners – 'we should just wait until he arrives.'

'Save a pile of dollars, Ethan,' the Gila Junction saloon owner said.

Bob Latchford's sigh was not his first sigh of the day, but it was certainly the longest. His feeling that big trouble was on the way sharpened to certainty.

The law office door opened. Hal Mannion stepped in, the Colt hanging on his hip looking as ridiculous and out of place as a good intention in Hell.

The thunder of horses being ridden hard followed him in. Through the open door Latchford saw Jody Crichton flash past, followed by a half-dozen riders, the toughest *hombres* the Crichton ranch had on its books. And, judging by the distance to their halt, Latchford guessed that they were piling into the saloon.

'Come to lend a hand, Bob,' Mannion said.

'Go on home, Hal,' Latchford snapped.

'Home?'

Hal Mannion had been clearly offended by Latchford's testy rejection of his services.

The marshal placated, 'If trouble comes, Hal...'

'Well, Marshal,' Mannion spat, 'I might not be of a mind to offer my services then!'

On his departure, Hal Mannion slammed the door hard enough to shift the law office floor. But Latchford was glad he was gone. The last thing he wanted was to see Mary Mannion wearing widow's weeds. And with the forces lining up in Bowen Crossing, the odds on that happening had shortened considerably.

Cy Brodie and the Apache were now within touching distance. Cy's next move could determine whether he would ride on, or become another parcel of bleached bones in the desert.

'Whiskey,' Jody Crichton ordered, grabbing the bottle from the barkeep. 'Belly up, fellas,' he invited his men.

He stalked off to sit in a corner all alone, brooding, his anger building by the second. When word had reached him about Ike Brown's demise, he knew then that if he wanted to stop Kate Trent marrying Latchford, he would have to do his own dirty work. Being a man who had learned from his father that bought services, connivery and trickery were the rungs on the ladder to safe prosperity, Jody Crichton had always followed his father's advice. But it was now too late to find someone else to do his killing for him. He knew that once he gunned down Bob Latchford, Kate Trent would despise him. But he would have to gamble on the future taking care of itself. Because if he did not act, and act swiftly, he had no future at all.

He had heard rumour that the wedding was off. However, being a suspicious man, he reckoned that such a tale might be a ruse to fool him until it was too late to do anything about it. Latchford knew how he felt about Kate – the whole damn territory did, so it made sense that such a rumour would be started to avert any trouble that he might be of a mind to stir. Safer, he had reasoned, not to take a chance. He simply could not believe that any man could pass on the chance to make Kate Trent his property.

The Apache's knife flashed past, inches from Cy Brodie's face. Brodie's fist went in the opposite direction to connect hammer hard against the side of the Indian's head. The jolt from the blow shot upwards into Brodie's shoulder. He clenched his teeth to absorb the pain. The stunned Apache reeled backwards, his eyes dancing to meet each other. It was a disappointment to Brodie to see the Indian not only stay on his feet, but to athletically use a boulder to spring back at him.

The hunting knife slashed back and forth. Cy was forced back, giving him no time to pick his steps. A rock slid from under his right foot and he went down on one hand. As bad luck would have it, it was the arm which was still soaking up the pain of the blow he'd landed on the Apache moments before. It buckled and he fell heavily. Losing no time to grasp his opportunity to finish Brodie off, the Indian lunged at him. Brodie's knee shot up. Fortune favoured the outlaw as his upraised knee connected with the Apache's groin. The Indian howled in pain. Bile spewed from his mouth as he doubled over.

Cy sprang to his feet and threw himself at the Indian, hoping that the Apache would be too concerned with his pain to impale him on the knife he still clutched. As he fell on the Apache, the upturned glint of steel told Cy that the Indian had both the time and the wits. Cy tried desperately to veer away from the waiting blade, but his committed lunge left no room for manoeuvre.

Cy Brodie's luck had run its course.

He was about to become buzzard bait.

## CHAPTER SEVENTEEN

*Rrrrrrrrr!*

The Apache glanced wide-eyed at the rattler only feet away from him, its ugly head raised and ready to strike. He flung himself aside, the immediate danger from the rattler having a greater priority than impaling the white man. With any luck, the white man would crash to the ground well within the rattler's spitting range. It was not a satisfactory outcome to the skirmish, but it was certainly preferable to losing all together.

He would still scalp him.

For a confused moment, until he saw the rattlesnake, Cy Brodie was at a loss to comprehend why the Apache would forfeit the advantage he enjoyed. The fear of dying by snake bite, which he had carried with him since childhood when he had seen a man die in that way, near stopped Brodie's heart.

With the Indian out of range, the snake's vile head darted Cy's way. Brodie spread his hands, palms down, in the hope that he might be able to spring aside and away from the rattler. It was a wild gamble, but it was a gamble he had to take. And if he was to survive for a while longer, it was a gamble he had to win.

He felt the shale bite into his palms. He cried out at the awful pressure on his arms as they supported his entire body weight, and he feared that his shoulders would be yanked from their sockets. His lower body was falling, dragging him down. He would crash to the ground on top of the snake or too near to it to survive. Cy put every last smidgen of his energy into one final somersault.

As his world went topsy-turvy, he could not believe his eyes.

Gabby Scanell was clawing his way up the side of Cy's horse, clutching fingers trying to reach the rifle in the saddle scabbard. Cy had a flashing thought about the odds turning in his favour, until he thought about the end result if Gabby succeeded in getting his hands on the rifle and firing it.

Cy crashed on to the rocky ground, and soaked up the punishment of a hundred rocks digging into his body. He was alive, and that's all that mattered. But for how long?

The Indian, awed by Brodie's spectacular acrobatics, soon gathered his wits and leaped on to Cy's back. He grabbed Brodie's hair and yanked his head back, exposing the outlaw's throat to the blade of the hunting knife.

'Hold it!'

Gabby Scanell's voice was the nearest thing to a frog croaking, but it held a menace that stayed the Apache's hand.

Gabby was leaning against the horse's left haunch for support, his eyes fevered and confused. His shoulders heaved with the effort of breathing, and his legs were seconds away from buckling. 'Step aside,' he ordered the Indian.

The Apache might not understand the old man's lingo, but there was no mistaking his message. He let go of Cy Brodie and edged back a safe distance, eyes furtive. He waited, ready to pounce when Gabby passed out, which would not be long.

'Drop the blade,' Gabby commanded.

The Apache dropped the hunting knife.

Cy stepped forward. 'I'll take that rifle now, Gabby.'

Gabby Scanell's face contorted with rage.

'Move an inch and I'll let you have it in the gut, Carter,' he growled.

Carter. Who the hell was Carter?

'I've been waitin' to settle 'counts with you a long time, mister,' he told Cy.

It did not matter who Carter was; obviously someone in Gabby Scanell's past who had done him a wrong, and with whom he had a score to settle.

'I'm not Carter, Gabby,' Cy coaxed. 'This is me, Cy Brodie.'

'Don't know no Cy Brodie,' Gabby spat. 'You're Jack Carter, you lyin', whinin' bastard!'

The Apache, quick as snake spit to cotton on, pointed an accusing finger at Brodie.

'Carter. Kill.'

Gabby's see-sawing eyes took in the Indian.

'Carter. Kill!' the Apache urged Gabby.

Gabby swayed and his knees bent.

'Me, kill,' the Indian offered.

Gabby, fury contorting his face, growled, 'Carter. Time you paid!'

Cy Brodie tensed. The Apache leered, smug, until Gabby swung the rifle his way.

'I've waited a hell of a long time to kill you, Jack Carter.'

'No Carter!' the Indian whined.

Though sweet, Cy Brodie's relief was short lived. If Gabby fired the rifle they would both be walking dead men.

Cy flung himself at Gabby. The rifle clattered to the ground but, thankfully, remained silent. The Apache sprang at Cy. Brodie grabbed the rifle and side swiped the Indian. The blow staggered him. Brodie followed through with a balled fist. The Apache reeled, but he remained upright. Cy spun the Indian round. He placed his left hand on the back of the Apache's head, and his right hand under his jaw. He jerked. The Indian's neck snapped.

Unconscious and dead weight, Cy hauled Gabby back on to the sled and resumed his trek to Bowen Crossing, worried that the sled, which had taken severe punishment, would disintegrate.

The terrain ahead seemed to hold no further threat. But Brodie knew that the desert often lured a man into a sense of false security prior to springing a surprise.

Often a fatal surprise...

# CHAPTER EIGHTEEN

Bob Latchford closed his eyes, pondering on the fickleness of life. Only yesterday he had the world at his feet, and today his future looked bleaker than a winter landscape.

'Bob...'

Latchford's eyes shot open.

'Kate!' He jumped up out of his chair and took her in his arms. 'You're a sight for sore eyes.' His joy turned to heart break when she turned away from his kiss and took a couple of paces back, clearly marking ground which he must not cross. Angered, Latchford asked, 'Did you ever love me, Kate?'

Kate's reply was every bit as angry. 'How can you doubt that I did, Bob?'

'Right now,' he growled, 'it's easy. A sniff of Cy Brodie, and you turn as cold in my arms as a damn corpse!'

'I won't deny that if Cy rode in that my heart wouldn't race some, Bob,' she admitted. Latchford grunted, his argument won. 'But I'm not sure if my heart wouldn't race for you faster still.' Latchford's blue eyes lit with surprise and no small amount of pleasure. However, both emotions were short lived when Kate elaborated. 'So, I reckon that it would only be fair to both you and Cy if–'

The lawman's anger returned full blown. 'You can have Cy Brodie, Kate. Maybe you two deserve each other.'

Tears dulled Kate Trent's eyes at the stinging attack.

'Are you saying that you wouldn't have me now anyway, Bob?'

Latchford considered. He let out a long sigh. 'I guess that's what I am saying, Kate.' Wearily, he said, 'Don't you see? How could I ever be certain that it was me you truly loved?'

'When Cy shows you'll know for sure, Bob.'

'If he shows,' the marshal said. 'And if he doesn't, Kate?'

'Then, I guess I'll go to my grave an old maid.'

The explosion of a gun sent Latchford diving for the gunrack behind his desk. He grabbed a shotgun, broke it, and slotted home two loads. He put a fistful of shells in his pocket, and hurried from the office as the sound of another gunshot rolled over the town.

'Stay here, Kate,' he ordered.

'Bob...'

The law office door slammed shut.

'...be careful,' Kate murmured.

Cy Brodie paused to watch the swooping vultures not far ahead, in fact close to the creek which was full of fond memories for him; the creek where he had first set eyes on Kate Trent. He was on the last leg of his trek to Bowen Crossing. Gabby Scanell was still drawing breath, but just about. He clung to the hope that he would be on time for Doc Hockley to work his magic on the old man.

Though the threat of the desert was behind him, Brodie knew that he had stepped from danger into even greater danger, shortening his journey by crossing Crichton range. If discovered by Crichton men, a rope over the nearest tree branch would be his fate.

Cy wondered about the swooping vultures. Probably a stray down. It happened all the time. But Brodie found himself inexplicably drawn to the spot where the vultures were massing, his blood chilling a little more with every inch travelled as his

138

apprehension grew.

'Well, if it ain't the Marshal, fellas,' Jody Crichton drunkenly declared, when Bob Latchford stepped cautiously through the saloon's batwings.

Latchford's glance went to the man lying on the floor at the far end of the long bar, a dark pool spreading out from under him. Andy Farley was the town drunk. The man standing over Farley, Jack Spottiswood, Jody Crichton's foreman, held a six-gun, a wisp of smoke curling from its barrel.

'Stole my drink, Marshal,' Spottiswood said, by way of explanation.

Latchford said, 'Andy was a nuisance, Spottiswood.' His voice dropped a notch. 'But not, I reckon, nuisance enough to kill him.'

Tension in the saloon hiked.

'I figure you should come to the jail until I think this incident through.'

The Crichton crew fell in behind their foreman.

'That a fact, Marshal? Well, I don't figure that way.'

Bob Latchford's gaze wandered across the Crichton crew. He patted the shotgun, and warned, 'Take this further, fellas, and some

139

of you will be heading skywards.'

Jody Crichton was in two minds as to whether he should let the confrontation develop. However, mindful of how Kate Trent would react, he decided against and told Spottiswood, 'Go with the marshal, Jack.'

Spottiswood and the crew were stunned and angered, until the rancher explained, 'There's no case against Jack.' Crichton's threatening gaze swept the saloon. 'Everyone here was a witness to Farley's aggravation.' He turned to Latchford. 'So, let's leave the marshal walk Jack to jail. Then, directly, we'll go and get him out. You have no case, Latchford. And you know it.'

He did.

'One day soon, Crichton,' Latchford promised, 'you'll run out of' – his eyes took in the saloon – 'cronies. I'll be right behind you when you do.'

Jody Crichton made an elaborate show of shaking in his boots. Latchford backed out of the saloon under a tirade of jibes and mocking laughter.

'You be careful now that you don't trip over that tail between your legs, Marshal,' Crichton called after him.

The laughter followed Latchford along the

boardwalk. He kicked out at a bucket outside the hardware store and sent it flying in front of him. When it landed, he kicked it again, even higher.

Relieved, Kate Trent said with a wry smile, 'You're in a mighty feisty mood for a man who has just kicked the bucket, Bob Latchford.'

At first he glowered at Kate, but was soon laughing along with her. Kate's fear drained away. Could she have felt such heart-stopping trepidation if she did not love Bob Latchford?

The stillness of the creek, other than the flapping of vulture wings, made Cy Brodie's approach a cautious one. Whatever interested the buzzards lay on a plateau above the creek. Brodie's heart quickened. The plateau was inaccessible to cattle, so the buzzards were not feasting on an unlucky cow.

What then?

Cy was faced with a dilemma. If he hitched his horse and made his way on foot, any predators about, such as mountain cats, might attack the mare. And if the horse was attacked, so would the helpless Gabby Scanell be. And if he stayed in the saddle, the clomp of the mare's hoofs on the rocks would announce his arrival long before he reached the plateau.

Deciding to make his approach on foot, Brodie hid his horse and Gabby's sled as best he could. He needed a view of Gabby Scanell which would allow for a clear shot, should any predators come sniffing around. That need ruled out using the thicker cover of the creek to hide the mare and sled.

He picked his steps carefully on his climb to the plateau, switching his glance between the plateau and Gabby. On reaching the plateau, Cy's stomach heaved on seeing the black feeding mass. He shooed the buzzards away. His heart sank on seeing Bull Rankin's staked-out body. Several knife blades had been drawn across his chest and belly. Not killer wounds – that would have been merciful – no, the purpose of the wounds was to let blood flow, just enough to scent the air and bring hungry predators calling. Rankin must have had a torturous wait. Cy Brodie hoped that his wait had not been too long.

The Apaches had extracted a terrible and vile price from Bull Rankin.

'Stranger comin'!' an old-timer sitting on the hotel porch called out, on seeing Cy Brodie on the edge of town. 'Got wounded in tow.'

On hearing the old man's cry, Bob Latchford stiffened. The rider was still some way off, but the marshal would have recognized the rider's gait anywhere. He had seen it often enough on Crichton range in the old days.

Cy Brodie was in town, and all hell would break loose.

## CHAPTER NINETEEN

Word buzzed. In seconds, the boardwalks were full, all eyes on Bob Latchford as Cy Brodie made his way along Main. The marshal settled the sixgun on his right hip, and stepped in to the street to block the outlaw's progress.

Cy Brodie dismounted. 'Howdy, Bob. How've you been?'

'Fine,' came Latchford's curt reply.

Brodie smiled. 'Looks that way. You've put on a pound or two.'

A rider thundered past, headed out of town. Latchford guessed that his destination was Kate Trent. The lawman's gaze came to rest on the unconscious Gabby Scanell.

'Must be near to hearing harp music,' he observed.

Cy nodded. He called out, 'Doc!'

The medico hurried from his office. After a cursory examination of Gabby Scanell, Hockley looked skywards and said, 'Needs more help than I can give him, Cy. You're welcome to put him in the infirmary until his time comes.'

'Thank you kindly, Doc,' Brodie said, 'but I've got other plans.'

'What kind of plans?' Latchford enquired tersely.

Cy Brodie mounted up.

'Hold it right there,' Latchford ordered. His hand hovered over his gun. 'You're not going anywhere, Cy. You've got unfinished business in this town.'

The tension on the boardwalks crackled.

'I'm not going far,' Cy said. 'Just as far as the hotel.'

'The hotel?'

'Yes.' The outlaw explained, 'Gabby Scanell dreamed of going to his Maker from the comfort of a four-poster bed. I figure that swanky suite in the hotel will do nicely. That done, I'll give you no trouble, Bob.'

As Cy Brodie rode the short distance to the

144

hotel, Latchford slipped into deep thought. Brodie's act of kindness and decency in walking into jail to help the old man, was clear evidence that he still possessed the kindly and fine ways which had marked him out as a man a cut above most.

The pain of locking up his former friend went deep inside Latchford.

'Are you going to let an outlaw make the rules, Marshal?' Ethan Briscoe called out.

Briscoe and his cronies had formed an unholy alliance with Jody Crichton, and they now crowded the boardwalk outside the saloon.

'I say string him up right now,' Jody Crichton shouted.

'Not before I get my money,' Briscoe said.

'I don't have any of your money, mister,' Cy Brodie said. 'Don't know what you're so all-fired up about a couple of hundred measly dollars for anyway.'

'Me neither,' Latchford added. 'Doesn't make sense all the trouble you're going to, Briscoe.'

The banker shifted uneasily under the lawman's stare, as did the Gila Junction men with him. 'If a banker is robbed and does nothing about it, he'll soon be robbed again,' Briscoe declared.

'Makes sense to me,' Jody Crichton piped up. 'So, let's hang Cy Brodie for rustling and bank robbery.'

Jack Spottiswood grabbed the lariat on his saddle. 'I've got the rope!'

Bob Latchford's bullet nipped at Spottiswood's toes caps. 'Stay right where you are, mister,' he warned. 'Cy Brodie is on his way to jail.'

'To bust out again?' Jody Crichton taunted.

Brodie continued on to the hotel, protected by Latchford's gun.

The desk clerk looked up in alarm when he saw his new scruffy guests. His alarm hiked when Cy Brodie asked for the key to the hotel's fanciest suite. He thought about protesting, but shelved his objection on seeing the grim purpose in the outlaw's eyes.

Bob Latchford arrived to help carry Gabby Scanell upstairs. When they had the old-timer settled in the four-poster, Doc Hockley arrived.

'I'll do what I can to see that your friend's passage into eternity will be as easy as possible,' the sawbones promised Cy.

'I thank you both for your charitable kindness,' Cy said.

Hockley lifted Gabby Scanell's right eyelid. 'Won't be a long wait,' he opined.

When Cy Brodie joined Bob Latchford at the room door to accompany him to jail, the lawman said, 'You come along to the jail when it's over, Cy.'

'I wish I could have avoided your town, Bob,' Cy said.

'Me, too,' Latchford growled, and left.

Not too far along the boardwalk after he had left the hotel, Bob Latchford made a decision which, for him, being the straight lawman he was, was a stark departure from the norm. He was turning in the door of the hardware store when Kate Trent's rig sped into town.

'If it's Cy Brodie you're looking for, Kate,' Latchford called, 'he's at the hotel.'

'The hotel?' Kate Trent's relief was palpable.

'For now,' Latchford added.

Kate's spirits slumped. She hesitated for a moment, caught between her desire to see Cy Brodie, and the hurt that her visit would cause Bob Latchford. It was with a heavy heart she headed to the hotel. Latchford almost changed his mind about the scheme he had concocted. But to his credit, he rose above his hurt and disappointment. He entered the hardware store.

'I need a saw,' he told the store clerk.

He left the hardware store and carried on to the livery.

'Your horse, Marshal?' the livery man enquired. 'You leaving town?'

Watching through the saloon window, Ethan Briscoe announced, 'Looks like the marshal is taking the easy option, gents.'

His cronies and the Crichton brood crowded to the window, disbelief being the common reaction.

Jody Crichton said, 'Never figured Latchford for a quitter.'

Briscoe chuckled smugly. 'Guess the odds against him have never been stacked higher before.' He glanced towards the hotel. 'Well, what're we waiting for?'

Bob Latchford did not go far, but the little way he went was almost too far.

His attention exclusively on Gabby Scanell's last words, Cy Brodie did not hear the room door open. Kate Trent hung back. Gabby's eyes lit up for the last time on seeing his plush surroundings. 'A darn four-poster,' he murmured breathlessly. Gabby Scanell's eyes. fluttered. He smiled weakly. 'Think I can hear them harps, Cy.' Gabby Scanell sank back on to his silk pillow and lay still.

Doc Hockley left the room quietly.

'Cy,' Kate called softly.

Brodie turned and looked for a long time at Kate, before she fled to his arms. Their embrace did not last long.

'Watch the stairs!'

Jody Crichton's harshly delivered order from the hall had Cy Brodie diving for his gun. He shoved Kate aside, just as the room door was kicked in, Spottiswood's gun blasting. Brodie, diving aside, shot the Crichton foreman between the eyes. The men behind him dived to either side of the door. Cy kicked it shut. He grabbed hold of Kate, kicked out the window and clambered on to the outside stairs, just as the room door was ripped apart by gunfire.

'The alley!' Crichton shouted.

Some of the men scattered down the stairs, others rushed to the shattered window to lay lead on Cy Brodie's tail. On seeing Kate fleeing with him, Crichton saw the danger she was in and ordered his men to hold their fire. He landed a fist in one man's face who continued shooting, and then tossed him head first out of the window.

Jody Crichton sped out of the room shouting, 'Hold your fire! Kate's with that bastard Brodie.'

The rancher need not have worried. Bob

Latchford, toting a shotgun, had the men cornered in the hotel foyer. All except one Crichton man who had arrived late in town, and was now creeping up from behind on the marshal. His gun butt scattered Bob Latchford's senses. The marshal slumped to the floor. Immediately, men were diving for the door.

'Hold up!' Crichton demanded.

But no one was listening.

As Kate and Cy fled past Doc Hockley's office, the door opened and the sawbones dragged Kate inside.

'Stay there, Kate,' Brodie ordered.

Men burst from the hotel door, guns blasting. Cy threw himself behind a cluster of sacks of flour outside the general store. The sacks of flour offered good cover, neutralizing the lead flying his way.

'Fan out,' Ethan Briscoe ordered the men.

Cy Brodie knew that once the men began coming at him from all directions, he had no hope of surviving the onslaught. It looked like he was going to end his career as an outlaw where it had begun.

With Kate Trent now out of the picture, Jody Crichton gave free and full rein to his spite.

'Flush out the bastard!'

Where, Cy Brodie wondered, had Bob Latchford got to?

Lead filled the air around Brodie, splintering wood and shattering glass. He lay flat on the boardwalk.

The sacks of flour behind which he had taken refuge were filled with the dull thud of bullets hitting them. They offered good cover, but with men now coming at him from both sides of the street, his chances of surviving the next couple of minutes were zero. Oh, he'd take a couple of men with him into eternity.

But having seen Kate Trent again, eternity was the last place Cy Brodie wanted to be.

## CHAPTER TWENTY

Inside the hotel, Bob Latchford stirred sluggishly, his muzzy senses slow to clear until the clerk's desk against which he was slumped was suddenly peppered by bullets. In seconds he was tuned into what was happening and had taken up a position in the hotel door, cutting loose with a shotgun blast that downed two Crichton hands and took the support beams for the hotel porch with it causing the porch roof to collapse at one end and leaving the remainder of the structure hanging by a thread.

Lead hotter than hell's coals splintered the hotel door and shattered its glass. Latchford ducked back inside to reload the shotgun, giving thanks that he had had the presence of mind to have pocketed a fistful of shells when he had gone to the saloon earlier to investigate Andy Farley's killing.

Shotgun reloaded, the marshal dived across the door, triggering the gun at two men making tracks to the hotel under covering gunfire to root him out. The shotgun blast tore a hole in the first man and continued on to do the same to his partner behind him.

Excited babble filled the street. Men ran for their horses, the lead-filled air of Bowen Crossing too dangerous for them now. Jody Crichton cursed and swore as his men dispersed.

Cy Brodie's gun opened up to kill the first man who made it to his horse, blasting him out of his saddle. A second man took a bullet in the gut and lay moaning in the street.

'Give it up, Crichton,' Latchford ordered.

However, the rancher was long past sanity and charged the hotel, six-gun spitting, leaving Bob Latchford with no choice but to defend himself. Jody Crichton stopped dead in his tracks looking at the bullet hole in his chest, mesmerized by the pulses of blood coming from the ragged hole, before he dropped to his knees and then onto his face in the dust.

Ethan Briscoe, paler than milk, emerged from the hardware store door waving a white handkerchief.

The man whom Brodie had wounded called to the Gila Junction banker, 'I need doctoring, Ethan.'

Briscoe, too busy saving his own skin, ignored the injured man's cry. 'Ethan...' the wounded man pleaded.

Angered by the banker's disregard for his plight, he called to Latchford, 'You want to know why a couple of hundred dollars was so damn important, Marshal?'

'Shut up, you fool!' Briscoe snarled viciously.

The wounded man gave a gurgling laugh. Blood seeped through his lips. 'Makes no diff'rence to me, Briscoe. I'm done for.' He glared bitterly at the banker. 'You see,

Marshal,' he explained, 'we had to retrieve those dollars the Brodie gang heisted at all costs, because those bills are counterfeit.'

'Counterfeit?' Latchford questioned.

'Yes, Marshal. Briscoe had a stroke of luck. He crossed paths with a whiskey-thirsty Reb who told him about a plan the Confederacy had had to undermine the Union's economy by printing counterfeit dollars.

'The plan never got off the ground, because the soldiers escorting the printing press and plates were attacked and mostly wiped out by Indians. But this Reb knew where the press and plates were hidden...'

The puzzle of the printing press and stacks of paper Cy Brodie had seen in the small room off Briscoe's office in the Gila Junction bank was solved.

'When that mining outfit picked the Gila Junction bank to stash all that cash in, Briscoe thought up a scheme to replace their good dollars with duds. Time was short. He needed help. The men who rode in here provided that help. We didn't need much persuading. Gila Junction will soon be dust. We were looking for a way out.'

His breath shuddered.

'We planned on being a long way away when the mining company discovered that their dollars were about as useful as a holed water bucket, Then...'

The dying man's gaze settled on Cy Brodie.

'That handful of dollars you grabbed were duds. US dollars stand out in Mexico. If those counterfeit dollars were discovered too soon...'

Bob Latchford now had an answer as to why Ethan Briscoe had gone to so much trouble to retrieve so little.

The dying man returned his bitter gaze to the Gila Junction banker.

'I told you we should have hightailed it, Ethan. That we'd never get our hands on the Brodie gang. You wouldn't listen.'

A racking cough snatched the last of the man's breath away.

The game up, Ethan Briscoe asked Brodie, 'How did you find out about the Longshot Mining Company's plans anyway?'

Cy Brodie smiled. 'You've got a big mouth, mister. Big lips, too.'

Puzzled, the banker said, 'I don't understand?'

'You'll have a long time breaking rocks to figure it all out,' Latchford grunted. 'If they don't hang you, that is.' His gun included Cy Brodie. 'Time to head for the caboose, gents.'

Coming from Hockley's office, Kate Trent

pleaded, 'You can't jail Cy, Bob.'

Latchford's response was brusque, 'He's a wanted man, Kate.'

Kate watched helplessly as Cy Brodie was marched off to jail.

Bob Latchford slammed the cell door shut on Ethan Briscoe. He escorted Cy Brodie to a cell further along. As he shoved Brodie into the cell, he murmured, 'Get ready to hit me...'

Brodie was stunned.

'There's a shack at the south end of town. The town's kerosene supply is stored there. I've cut out a section of the back wall that you'll be able to kick out, when I start blasting at you.'

He handed him a box of lucifers.

'I've spilled kerosene on the floor. The shack will burn fast and furiously. Everyone will think that you've perished. Behind the shack there's a stand of timber. You'll find a saddled horse hitched there. I'll tell Kate to meet you at her place.'

He shoved Cy roughly ahead of him.

'Make it look good, Cy.'

'Watch it, will you?' Cy growled.

Latchford shoved the outlaw again, harder. Cy swung a fist that floored the marshal, and sprinted for the law-office door. Latchford

156

counted to ten before giving chase.

Kate Trent watched in alarm as Cy Brodie burst from the law office, followed moments later by Bob Latchford, six-gun bucking. She had no way of knowing that Latchford's shooting was purely for effect and was no threat to Cy.

The danger, Latchford knew, was that some eager citizen might lend a hand and down Brodie. In an effort to avoid such a tragedy, the marshal kept shouting at folk to stay indoors as he charged after the outlaw.

'Stop shooting, Bob,' Kate cried out.

Latchford brushed past her. In an aside he said, 'Go on home, Kate. Cy will be with you soon.'

'I don't understand–'

'Don't have to right now. Go!'

On reaching the shack, Cy Brodie dived inside. Seconds later the shack was peppered with lead. He struck a lucifer and dropped it on the kerosene-soaked floor. A *whoosh* of flame engulfed the shack, almost trapping him in its ferocity. He found the cut-out section of the back wall and kicked it out. Free of the inferno, he raced to the nearby trees. He vaulted on board the horse and galloped off to Kate Trent's place, where he waited.

Waited.

And waited...

Until he knew Kate was not coming.

Bob Latchford was nursing his sorrows when Kate stepped into the law office wearing her wedding dress. Stunned, he held his breath.

Kate took him in her arms, and said, 'Marshal, the preacher is waiting.'

Soon after sun-up, Cy Brodie buried Bull Rankin.

'Well, Bull,' he murmured, 'the deadlock which you reckoned had me imprisoned in outlawry has been broken by a good man.' He doffed his hat at the mound of fresh earth. 'Be seeing you, Bull.'

Cy Brodie mounted up and rode away. Headed for Montana.